Power Trip

Treasure Malian

Acknowledgements

Before anything I must thank God, for not giving up on me even when I felt like giving up on myself. Thank you for continuously showing me that by your grace anything is possible.

To my mother and grandmother; no amount of words can express how much I love and appreciate you both. Thank you for everything, the motivation, and the continuous support you guys show me. No matter what the endeavor was, and there has been a few, LOL you guys were always in my corner. I'm blessed beyond measure to have you two in my life.

My step dad, thanks for being there all these years. Love you.

All my siblings, I love you guys to pieces! Nyema and Promise thanks for all the late night Oovoo sessions, and motivation you guys gave me.

Janelle, thank you so much for all your support throughout the years. No matter what was asked of you, you were there. 10yrs of friendship down, a lifetime to go!

Hassan!!!! Thank you for your support, for test reading and encouraging me to keep going. I love you.

Asia (BHATI) love you guh, thanks for the support. Mika, thanks for everything. U got next sis.

All the readers & authors I have met on FB that gave me encouragement and feedback, I appreciate you.

#PPP & #TBRS !!! The ENTIRE team Authors and Readers, love is love!

THANK YOU! Raymond Francis, Envy_Seal, & David Weaver for seeing something in me, enough to bring me into your family. I won't let you guys down.

Demettrea, you already know what it is girl! Love you to pieces! Started from hey, now we here! Thank you for all the support, talks, laughs, writing sessions… everything! Can we get LLAO3 like now please!

Chrissy, Love you Twin! My vampire life partner, thanks for your support and feedback. Waiting on Harlem Princess!

Anjela & Sheri, thank you both for the support, Sheri thanks for being a listening ear. Anjela, you have been a listening ear, and bought me so much laughter. Thank you. Angelique Long, thank you so much for everything love.

My editor, Errica Roseby; THANK YOU!

Brittani Williams, Thank you for the cover!

Last but certainly not least, thanks to everyone who frowned upon the idea of me writing a book, everyone who didn't offer one encouraging word, and everyone who thought I couldn't do it. THIS IS FOR YOU!

Chapter One

Skye

It was the first day of the rest of my life. I was beginning my journey as a law student at Columbia University. I was a bit early for my contract law class, so I grabbed a seat in the first row, and began to tap my Christian Louboutin heels against the tiled floor. I waited patiently for the other students as well as the professor to arrive. As I watched the students begin to enter the class room I became nervous. I felt my hands start to perspire, and my palms got clammy. I couldn't quite understand why I was nervous. I was an A student throughout my undergraduate career at NYU, but I knew law school was a different ball game. However, I was completely ready for the daunting task that was before me. Finally, the professor had arrived. I reached over into my Louis Vuitton tote bag that rested on the seat next to me, and grabbed my Mac Book Pro. I wanted to be ready in case I needed to jot down any notes.

I watched attentively as the professor began his spiel about his expectations for the semester and his students. He spoke for twenty minutes before handing out the syllabus and dismissing us. Seeing as it was the first day of class, it was unlikely that professors kept the students for the entire time; I couldn't be happier about that. The entire class got up and made a quick exit through the door located in the back of the classroom. I, on the other hand was moving a bit slow, because I received a text from my best friend, Ariana. As I was engulfed in the text conversation she and I were having, I didn't notice the guy standing by the door. That is, until I walked right into him.

"Oh my, I'm sorry about that." I said, looking up from my phone.

I thought to myself that this guy was fine. He looked to be about 6'1, give or take an inch, with nice smooth caramel skin; he reminded me of Derrick Rose. He rocked a low cut with waves that made me want to go swimming. Being a fashionista, you know I had to scrutinize his attire. I must say the man could dress. He looked dapper in the YSL V-neck, slacks, and the Bally's that adorned his feet. I had to get out of my own thoughts when the stranger flashed me the sexiest smile I had ever seen; showing a perfect set of pearly whites.

"It's aight beautiful, I'm not made of glass."

There was suaveness in his tone, which had piqued my interest. I was far from a thirsty chick though, so I smiled back and walked away. We had class together so we definitely would cross paths again.

As I walked past him I could feel him staring; more like burning a hole in my back. It was expected though because I'm bad. I have gorgeous exotic features, with a set of hazel eyes that would mesmerize anyone who looked into them, even if only for a second. I'm shaped nicely; I could definitely be one of them chicks in a Lil Wayne video or something, but much classier though. I'm equipped with a flat tummy, thick thighs, big butt, and a set of 36 C boobs that were perky and sat upright. How could I blame him for staring?

As I walked across campus to where I parked my BMW M5, I thought about the stranger. There was something about his smile and his demeanor that made me want to know more. My thoughts were interrupted by the ringing of my cell phone. I had to push the thoughts about the stranger to the back of my mind; well, for now at least. I slid my finger across the screen of my iPhone to answer.

"Hey, mom, wassup?"

My mother and I are extremely close. We speak everyday about any and everything under the sun.

"Hi, baby girl. How was your first day?"

I could tell my mother was extremely happy that I decided to follow her path into the law field. She couldn't hide the enthusiasm in her voice as she waited to hear about my first day of law school.

"Mom it went pretty well. I'm looking forward to the rest of the semester. The classes I'm taking this semester seem really interesting, so yea, we'll see how it goes."

I finally reached my car when I felt a hand tap me on the shoulder. I turned around and was pleasantly surprised that it was the stranger. I put up one finger, signaling him to give me a minute to wrap up my conversation. I had completely missed the last thing my mother said, and knew it wouldn't be smart to let her know I was no longer focused on what she was saying. I thought it would be a good idea to just end the conversation.

"Mom, it's still early. I'mma drop by your office so we can grab lunch. Love you."

I quickly ended the call and focused my attention back on the mystery man.

I gave him a once over before speaking. "So, you following me?"

He let out a smooth chuckle and smiled. Damn I really wished he would stop giving me that sexy ass smile.

"Nah, it's not even like that. I'm just the type of nigga that goes after something that I want."

Who did this nigga think he was? Better question, who did he think I was?

"Oh, I see. So what exactly is it that you want uhh…?" Here he was declaring that he was after something and we didn't even know each other's name.

"Cameron; just Cam is cool."

I extended my hand for him to shake it. "Nice to meet you Cameron, I'm Skye."

The electricity that shot through my body the moment our hands touched was mind boggling. What was it about this man? Whatever it was, I was ready to find out.

"So Wassup? I was hoping we could exchange numbers and get together tonight..."

I had to cut him off. "Tonight? You don't waste anytime do you?"

Realizing my hand was still in his, I slowly pulled it out of his grasp.

"I told you, Skye, I go after what I want. I already know that I'm interested in getting to know you, and obviously we on the same page because you're still here."

I had to admit that Cameron was right. I was definitely interested in getting to know him. Without out any further inquiry, we were swapping numbers. I handed him his phone back after saving my number. What he did next was shocking, and left my heart racing. Cameron moved closer and kissed me on the forehead.

"Drive safe and don't forget to call me."

With that said, he was gone. I watched for a few minutes as he disappeared back into the university's court yard, before jumping in my car and heading down town to my mother's job.

****

My mother was one of the top criminal attorneys in the state of NY. I admired everything about her; her strength, determination, her resilience, and her success. She was the definition of "Started from the bottom, now we here!" She grew up in Brooklyn; Marcy Projects to be exact. No one expected her to be where she was today. However, she refused to let the negative opinions of a few, and the drug infested housing projects determine who she would ultimately become. With that being said, once she got her working papers at the young age of fifteen, she hit the ground running. She was on her grind day in and out, doing any odd job she could snag, and still managed to keep way above average grades in school.

While girls her age were out partying and turning up, my mother was working, or in her books. It paid off too, because she graduated high school at the age of sixteen and started college that following fall at Howard University. Till this day she will tell you, leaving Brooklyn to attend school in Washington, D.C. was one of the best decisions of her life. Not just because the opportunities she was presented with at Howard, but because that's where she met my father, Harvey Lewis.

Yes, that Harvey; three time NBA champion, four time MVP Harvey Lewis. He and my mother met during a visit he took to Howard with his fraternity brothers. They love to tell the story of how they met and fell in love. Don't get me wrong it's a beautiful story, but it's also a little too long winded; I prefer the short version. They met, knew they wanted to be together, and although he went to Duke in North Carolina, and she was in D.C., they made it work. They came from different walks of life; my father too was born and raised in Brooklyn, but his circumstances were different. He was from Park Slope, an uppity neighborhood, and he came from a home with two parents who were pretty well off, seeing as they were both doctors. He never let the difference in their upbringing come between what he and my mother shared. It worked out well, because I came into the world four years later.

My parents adored me. As far back as I can remember I never wanted, or needed for anything. I was their princess, and was treated accordingly; still am. I had the best of everything, went to the best schools, rocked the best designers, you name it. I am forever grateful for my parents and the life they provided for me. I turned out to be a mixture of the both of them. I got my exotic looks from my mother, and in addition to that, her drive and ambition. My father blessed me with this fiery attitude and no nonsense personality. He was never one to be fucked with, and neither am I. I hate that people see a pretty face, designer clothes, hear a soft voice, and assume I'm soft. Let's not get it twisted, I may have been raised with a silver spoon in my mouth, but I was far from oblivious to the things that went on around me.

****

Every time I visit my mother's office, I reflect on our life. The photos she had strategically placed around her office were like a time line of all the major events and points in her life. I continued to look at all the photos as I'd done a dozen times, before she finally came waltzing through her office door. My mother walked over to me and embraced me before stepping behind her desk.

"Hi Beauty." My Mom said to me as she dropped a thick manila envelope on the desk and took her seat.

The sunlight coming through the window radiated on my mother's smooth caramel complexion. She was a very pretty woman; didn't look a day over 25 although she was 41. I pray that I look as good as she does when I reach her age.

"Hey mommy. We still doing lunch or are your swamped?"

She gave me a face that answered my question. It was rare that my mother had time for anything other than her cases because she was just that good. I figured she wouldn't be able to leave the office for lunch. It was cool though, I respected her grind.

"Don't even worry about it, Mommy. Rain check?" I smiled at her to reassure her that it was okay.

"You should come over tonight. Your dad and I would love to have dinner with our only child."

I wanted to take her up on that offer. The time I spent with my parents was invaluable, and I loved to get with them every chance I got. However, I already told Ariana I would go with her to Green House for some party that Brooklyn rapper, Fabolous was hosting.

"Tonight I'm heading out with, Ari mom, but tomorrow for sure."

My mom was about to respond, but her phone started ringing.

"Go ahead mom get that I'm going to head out. I'll call you later on."

We sent air kisses and I left.

****

I hadn't had a bite to eat all day so my first stop was Habana Outpost. I absolutely love their Cuban sandwiches and margaritas. I had to pass on the margarita since I was driving but I definitely enjoyed my Cuban. I had some time to kill so I decided to hit 5th avenue, and do some shopping for the night that was ahead.

Cameron

There I was, trying to get through this meeting with my pops, and my thoughts kept drifting to shorty I met at my school. I was in no way, shape, or form the nigga that chased bitches, but it's something about shorty. I wanted Skye, and Imma have her.

"Yo, Cam, pay attention."

I guess my pops could tell that my mind was elsewhere. Not that I really needed to hear him out. I knew what he was saying and I personally felt the shit didn't apply to me. My pops' had a bunch of little niggas working for him who needed to be reprimanded, and I definitely wasn't one of them.

"I hear you, Pops." I had to say something so he would think that I was listening.

To keep it trill, the only thing on mind at that moment was shorty. Why though? That shit was tripping me out. My pops went on for a good two hours, which was expected, because it was the monthly meeting where everyone who was somebody in the organization, got together to catch up and touch bases. I looked around at the familiar faces and smiled to myself. These niggas were my family, and proved themselves to be loyal on more than one occasion. Majority of them had shit on lock with my pops since before I was born, and was still riding. I put a few of my niggas on too, just because any real nigga would make sure that his niggas 'was eating. That was me; as real as they come. Niggas knew not to let my suit and tie fool them. I was good at gun play when my hand was forced. It rarely ever came to that though; that's what I had all those niggas for.

I thought about how shorty might react to my lifestyle. Not every day you meet a nigga in law school who was knee deep in the drug game. I'm a different type of dude though. From the day I graduated from high school, my pops was ready for me to dive head first into the game. Shit, one day the entire operation would be under my reign. I had no problem with that, but I did have a few stipulations of my own. I told my pops I was going to college, and ultimately law school. Don't get me wrong, I could never really see myself as a nine to five nigga, but I knew the advantage that having an education would give me in this game. A Law education at that. I knew shit, and continued to learn shit that niggas wouldn't even think about until they were standing before a judge getting the book thrown at them.

I had to laugh at myself though. Nobody outside this organization knew that I had any involvement in it, and I wasn't about to change that for a chick. I no longer needed to think about how she would react, because she would never find out. Shit, not even my mom's knew about the shit I was into. Speaking of my mother, I missed her, I made a mental note to head out to Long Island as soon as time permitted, to spend some much needed time with my favorite lady.

The meeting had been concluded for a minute, but niggas was still lounging around kicking it. I had some loud that I was in the mood to blow, so me and my nigga Ty rolled up and got bent. We were on the forth blunt when my iPhone started vibrating in my pocket. I pulled it out and watched as Shorty's named flashed on my screen. As bad as I wanted to talk to Skye, she was gonna have to wait. I sat my phone on the table and enjoyed my high.

"My nigga, what you doing tonight?"
I heard Ty talking which made me open my eyes and sit up.
"Hopefully Imma be doing this bad ass shorty I met at school today."

We laughed and gave each other dap. Ty was my nigga, more like my brother. We been niggas since we came out womb; our pops were right hands. We did everything together: fought, fucked bitches, got money, you name it. I knew that besides my pops, this was the only nigga walking the earth I could trust with my life. My phone vibrated again, but this time it was text.

"Hey wassup. I know you wanted to meet up tonight, but I promised my best friend I would roll with her to Green House. You're welcome to come if you want. Talk to you later."

"Yo, Ty, you want to mob to Green House tonight?" I tapped this nigga who looked like he was about to pass out and shit.

"Yea, I heard Fab hosting some shit there. You know where ever that nigga at, a shit load of bitches will follow."

I laughed at the truth behind his statement.

"I thought you was trynna see shorty though." Ty asked as he switched positions in his seat.

That nigga always wanted to get comfortable and sleep when he was high. I laughed. "Yea, Skye the one who told me to come through. She going with her best friend."

Hearing shorty had a friend put this nigga on full alert again. "Her friend better be bad, you always get the A1 chicks and leave me with the ugly ass friend."

I couldn't say much to that, it was true.

****

As we pulled up to Green House, I knew I made the right decision by having my driver bring us. Finding parking would have been impossible, and I didn't have the patience for that shit. When the Range came to a complete stop, I secured my nine that was tucked in the small of my back. I doubted highly that niggas would need to pop off at the venue, but I don't take chances with my life. I hoped out the whip with Ty and my muscle, Rick and Max. Those niggas are the definition of loyal. They would bust shots and take shots for me need be so I make it my business to keep them close.

"Cameron!"

As we got closer to the entrance I heard someone call out my name. I already knew who the voice belonged to. Two people on the Earth called me Cameron: my mother and

Skye. I knew my mother wasn't there to see that nigga Fab, so it had to be the latter. I looked toward where the voice was coming from and saw she was standing at the entrance with the bouncers and another shorty. The sight of shorty made my dick jump. Skye had her hair up in one of them messy buns that bitches seem to love so much, but the shit looked perfect on her. I really got to see her features, and she looked better than she did earlier that day. Her friend wasn't bad looking either. I smiled at her and pulled her close to me once I reached her.

"Wassup, beautiful?" I said as I wrapped my arms around her for a hug.

"Hey, this my best friend, Ariana." Skye introduced me to her home girl.

"What up, this my brother, Ty, and my niggas Rick and Max."

Her home girl's eyes fell on Ty, and she blushed. I looked over at him, and that nigga was in a trance too. Ol love at first sight ass nigga.

"I know we not getting in these long ass lines." I said, looking at the lines that seemed to wrap around the corner.

Skye and her home girl laughed, but I was dead ass serious.

"No, Jay they with us." Ariana said to the bouncer.

He nodded his head and let us walk in.

"Oh they got some clout and shit." I thought to myself.

We followed the ladies to their section and took our seats. I ordered bottles to jump start the evening.

"You look good, ma." I had to let Skye know she was definitely killing the game tonight. "Thanks" she said, standing up. "Come dance with me."

Did I hear shorty right? Do I look like a nigga that dance?

"I'm straight, ma. Go ahead though. Let me watch you."

She turned to walk away with Ariana as Rich Gang's "Tap Out" came blaring through the speakers. I watched as she sang the hook along with Future and danced.

"Skye is bad son." Ty said, throwing back his Patron.

"I told you fam. Her home girl a little cute too."

I had to throw that in there since he complains that he gets stuck with the ugly bitches. I turned my attention back to Skye. Watching her dance made me wanna just fuck her on the dance floor. When French Montana's "Pop That" came on, I watched her twerk and bounce her ass. I couldn't help myself; I found myself creeping up behind her and grabbing her waist. Skye turned her head, and when she saw it was me, she continued to bounce on my dick.

"I thought you didn't dance." Skye said, giggling.

I palmed her ass and said "I didn't wanna miss out on this."

****

The rest of the night was straight. We got drunk, danced, and talked. By the time we dipped out the spot it was almost 4:00am. I wanted to take shorty back to my crib, but something told me to chill and let shit between us run its own course. I was really feeling her. Skye wasn't just a pretty face. She was mad cool, smart, and didn't seem thirsty. You could tell she was feeling the kid, but she wasn't being overly obvious like some of these chicks are now a days.

"I had a good time, Cameron, Thanks for coming to chill with us."

Yo, even her voice was sexy.

"I did too, and it's nothing ma. Thanks for the invite. You drove?"

I looked around for the white X5 Skye hopped in earlier, but I didn't see it.

"Nah, I knew parking would be disastrous. I took a cab."

I looked at her sideways. "A cab? It's almost four in the morning, ma. You not about to catch a cab home. I'm not with that.

I walked over to where Ariana and Ty were talking, with Skye on my heels.

"Yo, Ariana, you drove here?" I questioned.

"Yea I did. I'mma take Skye home, don't worry."

I was gonna interrupt because I had a better idea, but Skye beat me to it.

"Ya'll acting like I live far. I can…"

I interrupted her, "Nah it's quiet for that. Ty, what you about to get into bro?"

I had a feeling Ty was sliding off with Ariana, and I was never one to cock block.

"I'm straight, bro. I'll hit you later on."

That's my nigga. I was a proud big bro. I wanted to see if I would be as lucky.

"Aight, son. Yo, Ari, it was nice meeting you ma. Skye, my driver can take you home."

I paused to see if Skye would object, but she didn't. She hugged her home girl, said goodbye and followed me, Rick, and Max to the car.

****

When we pulled up to the address shorty gave my driver, it was the Waldorf Astoria. Shorty must have really been caking to live like that. Who was this girl? I hopped out the truck and held the door open for her.

"This how you living shorty?"

She smiled "It seems that way, but thank you for the ride; and for tonight. I had a good time. Get home safe."

I started to speak as I hugged her "No problem, Shorty. Oh and I'm not going home yet… gonna find a spot for some food, cause a nigga starving. Good night though."

I turned around walked back to the car and Skye called after me.

"Cameron, I mean if your boys don't mind waiting or coming back for you, you can come up. I can cook."

She didn't need to tell me twice. I dismissed my boys and followed behind Skye to her place.

Shorty crib was dope; she definitely had taste. She told me I could look around and make myself comfortable while she jumped in the shower, so that's what I did. I looked at the pictures she had hanging up in her living room; seemed like she came from a cool family. I spotted a picture of her and Harvey Lewis.

"Damn shorty mess with old ball players? Fuck this picture shit, I should go jump in the shower with shorty. Nah, let me chill."

I walked over to the cream sectional and sat down. I sat back with my eyes closed and relaxed. Shit felt good because a nigga was low key tired.

Skye

That shower was everything I needed and more. I stepped out feeling like a new person as I walked into my bedroom that was adjacent to my bathroom. I dried off, slipped on a pair of Victoria Secret lace panties, and applied some Dove lotion. I sat rubbing my legs for a minute, just because I loved how smooth they were. Then I remembered I had Cameron waiting. I slipped on a pair of boy shorts and a wife beater, and pranced into the living room.

"Really? Did this boy really fall asleep?"

I stood in front of the couch shaking my head. He was fine as fuck, even when he slept. I smiled to myself. I grabbed the throw blanket that was folded across the arm of the couch, and put it over him before heading back to my room and retiring to my bed.

****

The next morning, I woke up feeling rejuvenated. I glanced at the neon numbers on the cable box which read 10:13. I felt like lying there for another hour or two, but decided to get up and make breakfast, since the original plan was for me to cook. I climbed out of bed stretching my 5'4" inch frame as high as it could go, before entering the bathroom to wash my face and brush my teeth. After brushing my jibs, I looked myself over in the mirror. My bun was extremely messy but still cute, so I left it as is and headed to started breakfast.

As I opened my bedroom door, the aroma of good cooking hit me and my stomach growled.

Did he make me breakfast?

I headed to the kitchen to find Cameron fixing our plates on the center island top. Wow that was really nice of him. I stood and admired him doing his thing.

When he finally sensed my presence, he looked up and flashed his panty wetting smile and said "Good Morning ma. I was gonna wake you up in a few. I figured you would be hungry when you woke up, so I found my way around your kitchen."

I got closer and saw Cameron made pancakes, eggs, and bacon. I took a seat across from where he was standing.

"You didn't have to, but thanks though. I really appreciate it. And sorry for not waking you up last night. I thought you were tired so I left you alone. Well, obviously you were, because you were passed out."

He laughed, sat down to join me, and we ate. After breakfast I gave him a wash cloth and toothbrush, and let him go handle his business while I cleaned up the kitchen. I was sitting at the island drinking a bottle of water when he came and joined me.

"I called Ty. He'll be here in a minute to get me and you'll have your space back."

I looked up at him and rolled my eyes. Damn, I hope he didn't notice that.

"Dang, you acting like I'm kicking you out."

I kind of wanted him to spend the day with me.

"Nah, it's not like that. I need to change and shit; I can come back if you want."

I thought it about for a second. Hell yea I wanted him to come back, but I wasn't about to seem that eager.

"I mean it's whatever. I guess we'll catch up another day or something."

He shook his head side to side and sighed. "Come on Skye, you can keep it trill with me, ma. If you want me to stay, say that. No need to hide how you feel and shit."

Cameron was right; I didn't need to because he either was gonna respect it or not.

"Yeah, I want you to stay. I mean you slept in my house, and I barely know anything about you. However, I do understand that you want to go home and change, and that's fine."

I stood up and put the water bottle in the recycle trash before walking out the kitchen.

Call it being a brat if you want, but I'm used to getting everything my way. If he knew I wanted him to stay, that's what he need to do. I sat down in the lazy boy; my favorite chair ever because it was just so comfortable and big. It swallowed me when I sat down, and that's what I liked most about it. I grabbed the remote off the coffee table and turned on the TV. I started flipping through the channels, wondering when he was going to come in the living room after me, but he didn't until he was coming to say bye because Ty had arrived.

****

Since the day at my house, I hadn't really talked to Cameron. Of course I saw him during class, but that's about it. I guess he wasn't feeling that I was being a brat about him leaving, but whatever. That is Skye, all day, every day; never change, just like Jay-Z said in his song. If he was going to deal with me, he better learn to get with it. Besides, I haven't really had the time to think about him. It's only week three of classes, and I was becoming a bit overwhelmed. Law school is really no joke. Seems like the only thing I have time for nowadays is school and seeing my parents. I haven't even hung out with Ariana, but that's not because of schedule conflicts. It's because her and Ty been connected at the hip since the night we went to Green House. I'm not mad though. He's a cool dude, and they seem to really enjoy each other's company.

That night was turning out to be no different than my past few nights. There I was, sitting on my living room floor, surrounded by books, in a pair of boy shorts and a baggy off the shoulder t-shirt. I don't care how it sounded, I was comfortable. I kept looking back and forth between my legal writing text book, and contracts text book. Those classes were going to be the death of me. How did my mother do this? Shit, not only did she finish law school with honors, she did it while raising a baby. I was like four when she graduated.

I flipped back and forth continuously, becoming more restless as the minutes seemed to get away from me. I was at the point where I was ready to toss my text books aside and hit the bed, when my bell started ringing. I definitely wasn't expecting anyone, so it startled me a bit. I figured that maybe it was Ariana stopping by. Other than my parents, she was the only one with permission to come over whenever she wanted. I got up from the floor and walked to the front door. I opened the door, and was in for the shock of my life when I saw Cameron standing there with orange roses. I honestly don't like roses because they stink to me, but orange is my favorite color. How did he know that?

I stood there looking at him for a minute before he spoke breaking the silence.

"You going to let me in or not?"

I didn't answer, just moved to the side, giving him space to come in. Once he was inside, I closed the door and turned to him. Cameron handed me the flowers and went to kiss my forehead, but I moved.

"Thanks!" I said as I headed to the kitchen to put the flowers in some water.

I didn't expect him to follow me since he didn't the last time he was there, but surprise, surprise, he did.

"You don't want to be bothered?"

Did he really just ask me that?

As if we didn't have class together for three weeks, and he chose not to speak one word to me.

"I never said that, but wassup though. What brings you by?"

I sat on the stool and he sat across from me, staring into my eyes. I felt myself blush, so I turned my head.

"I just wanted to see you. I know I should of reached out or spoke to you when I saw you in class and shit, but it's just that…"

I cut him off. "You don't really need to explain yourself to me. It's cool."

I could care less why he didn't speak to me, because to me regardless of what his reasoning was, it was petty as hell.

We sat in silence for a few more minutes until he decided to speak again.

"I just want you to keep it trill with me all the times. I'm not a regular nigga, Skye. Don't tell me shit because you think it's what I want to hear, or because you afraid of my reaction."

Whoa… afraid of his reaction? This nigga got the game fucked up.

"First off Cameron, it wasn't even like that. I wasn't telling you what I thought you wanted to hear, nor was I afraid of your reaction. I just didn't deem it necessary for me to tell you that I wanted you to stay. You knew that! I guess you just wanted to hear me say it, but that's neither here nor there. Not speaking to me over that was petty."

By the time I finished my rant, Cameron was behind me, and spun the stool around. Now we're face to face.

"You're right, Skye. My apologies, I handled it wrong." He kissed me softly on my lips. "You forgive me?"

I was unable to answer. The kiss left me feeling some type of way. His lips were so soft and moist. Not moist where u think he walks around with slob all over his mouth, but just right; which was good because I would never tolerate dry lips. He lifted my chin with his finger, and looked me in my eyes. I looked back feeling like our souls were speaking to each other.

I finally was able to speak. "Yes, I forgive you, Cameron."

He smiled and stepped away from me. "What were you doing? In bed?"

I stood up and headed toward the living room, and he followed me.

I stood next to my textbooks and pointed. "This! Story of my life."

Cameron chuckled. I wanted to know what was funny. This school crap was stressing me out.

"You look stressed. Take a break lets kick it before I have to run. We can finally talk, get to know each other and shit."

I sat Indian style on the floor and picked up a text book. A break wasn't going to help me pass those classes, but I could multitask.

"What do you want to know?"

I watched as he sat down on the sectional and got comfortable.

"How old are you? How you know Harvey?"

I had to stop his interrogation. "Damn, are you interrogating me? I'm 21, and he's my father.

Cameron gave me the same reaction everyone else gives when I say Harvey is my dad, but I don't get it; he's an ex NBA player, not the president of the United States.

"Yea, so tell me Mr. Cameron, What are you about?" I shifted my focus to him, so he could see my interest in really knowing who he was.

"I mean what you see is basically what you get. I'm twenty-three, last year at Columbia, I'm from Harlem, regular shit."

I gave a face that must have told him that the little information that he volunteered wasn't going to cut it, so he went on. Cameron told me everything, at least I felt like it was everything. He grew up no different than me; his dad was a business man, and his mom was a stay at home wife and mother. I mean my mother didn't stay home, but in terms of coming from a good home and being well provided for, we had that in common. Cameron spoke about his little sister, and I could tell that she meant the world to him; a family man, that was a plus. He had a soft side to him, and I liked that. Yeah having a tough exterior was cool and all, but what female wanted a guy who she couldn't connect with on an emotional level. He didn't really dabble too much into the lives of his parents, which was fine. My intent was never to pry; I just want to know who I'm dealing with. You can't learn everything about a person in one night, and I didn't expect to. However, what I did learn helped me make the decision to keep seeing him.

I opened up to him, which was shocking. I normally kept my life story under wraps, but I felt comfortable with him. Just as he did, I shared with him a bit about my life growing up and a little about my family. Cameron was clearly as interested as I was. I was definitely looking forward to seeing where this relationship would go, if anywhere.

Chapter Two

Ty

Every year, Cam's parents have this nice ass Thanksgiving dinner party at their crib in Long Island, and this year was no different. My pops was coming through, and Ariana and her parents were too. I had to admit, I was really digging shorty. I was at the point where I wanted to let her in completely, but I couldn't. I didn't want to fuck up what my nigga had going on with Skye because he wasn't ready to tell her about his other life. As his boy, it was my job to protect his secrets at whatever cost. I didn't understand though, Cam and Sky been seeing each other as long as I been fucking with Ariana; like three months and shit. Everything seemed cool; they were always together between school, date nights, all night phone calls, and they were damn near inseparable. Whenever they weren't together, it was because Cam was in the street with me grinding. It seemed serious enough, so why not just be one hundred with shorty? It wasn't really my place to speak on though.

I snapped out my thoughts when I heard Mama Mariah calling me.

"Tyquan. Hello, Ty!"

She had to almost shout to get my attention.

"Yes, sorry, Mama. Wassup?" I answered, looking in her direction.

"Your guest Ariana and her parents are here."

I stood up to head to the door, and saw the look on Cam's face. He was trynna hide the fact that he was wondering where Skye was, but I know him.

"Okay, I'm coming now thanks, ma."

I walked toward the foyer and approached Ariana and her parents as they waited patiently by the door. Ariana's face lit up when she saw me, and even her mother smiled. She never met me before, but I figured anyone who could make her daughter happy deserved at least a smile from her.

"Hello, Mr. and Mrs. Morgan. Hey, Ari, you look beautiful."

I shook her father's hand, hugged her mother, and gave her a hug as well. They were cool; her pops spoke to me as if he already knew me. I guess Ari had been talking about me. I took them to the den where Cam's parents were, and introduced them. They seemed to hit it off and began to engage in conversation. Ariana and I dipped off back into the living room to join Cam. As we were walking through the foyer, the doorbell rang. I was already right there so I went to answer it. I opened the door and saw that it was Skye and her parents. Damn, her mom looked like she could be her twin. I thought Skye was bad, but her moms could get it if I wasn't feeling Ari and if she wasn't married... nah, even if she was married.

"Hey, Ty." Skye smiled at me as I moved to the side so they could come in.

Cam's parents were approaching the door just in time.

"Wassup, Skye. Hi Mr. and Miss Lewis. Let me get Cameron for y'all."

I took Ariana's hand in mine, and we walked off to get Cam. He must have been listening with his bionic ass ears, because that nigga was already walking toward us. I nodded my head at him as he walked past us. Once Ariana and I were seated in the family room, I texted my pops to see where he was at. I slid my phone back in my suit pants pocket and focused my attention on Ari.

"Yo sis." I called Cam's little sister Victoria, and took her attention away from whatever she was doing on her phone; probably texting.

"Yes, bro. Wassup?" She said, lifting her head.

"This Ariana. Ari that's Vic, Cam's little sister."

As the girls were exchanging hellos, Cam came into the living room and signaled for me to come here.

I kissed Ariana on the cheek. "I'll be right back ma."

I got up and followed him. We walked to the west wing of the house and took the elevator down to the bunker. I knew it was serious because we never went down there. Once inside the bunker, Cam walked over to the floor to ceiling safe that was built into the wall. I knew to stand back until he opened it. He did a few steps that I couldn't see, before punching in a code and opening the safe.

He looked over his shoulder and called out to me. "Come on, bro."

As I got closer, I could see that the safe was full of artillery; different types of guns, grenades, knives, you name it.

"What happened?" I almost regret asking the moment the words fell from my lips.

"They hit the warehouse in red hook and bodied Rick."

Cam's words hit me like a ton of bricks. Rick was like an uncle to us since we were little niggas. Whoever did this was about to feel the wrath of a lot of hurt people.

"Who the fuck is they? And what was there?" I paced the floor as I waited for answers.

Niggas like me didn't cry, but losing Rick was a hard pill to swallow. Even thugs cry, right? Fuck it though; I didn't have time to shed tears.

"Man and those niggas from Cypress. Crazy shit is that nobody knows about that warehouse except a very limited amount of people. So, somebody close is on some snake shit. As far as the loss we took…ten keys, and a half a mil."

Did I hear that nigga correctly? Ten fucking keys a half a mil? Nah, shit was about to be ugly for them East New York niggas.

"How we know who was behind it?"

Cam stood up holding a Mac 11; the machine gun happened to be his weapon of choice.

"My pops set up security cameras at all the spots, but only ones who know about the cameras is him, your pops, me, and now you. Max made it out and he called my pops a little while ago, then he sent your pops to the other spot out there to check the cameras."

That was probably why he didn't text me back yet. It was fucking Thanksgiving. Who does this this shit on

Thanksgiving? I thought about what was to come next while Cam kept talking.

"No cops showed up, as expected. The warehouse is so out of the way, so no one could pin point where the shots were coming from. The cleanup crew should be there now handling Rick's body, and whatever mess is left."

I didn't need to hear anything else. I stepped into the safe and grabbed two .45's.

"What's the plan?" I looked to Cam for answers.

"Max on his way to pick us up. We gonna ride through Cypress and send a little message. That nigga picked the wrong team to fuck with. I know he not gonna be out and about, but the good thing is that I know where his parents stay."

I knew it was on, and I was ready. Somebody had to pay for us losing a family member. If we had to put everybody in Cypress in the ground before we got to Man, so be it.

****

The ride to Cypress Hills was silent. Occasionally, Cam cursed because Skye was blowing up his phone. I understood he was in a different place, but he could have told shorty he had to run out. He just left her in the dark completely. Ariana wasn't blowing up my phone because I texted her a bullshit story about my pops' car not starting, and him needing a ride.

"You ready son?" Cam said, taking me out of my thoughts.

I looked out the window and noticed that we were in Cypress. Max pulled the car into a parking spot, and we all hopped out with hoods and ski masks on. We followed Cam into a building, then up to the third floor. We lined up on both sides of the hallway behind Cam as he knocked twice on the apartment door, with his hand covering the peephole. Seconds later, an elderly lady opened the door. Her eyes nearly popped out of her head as she watched five masked men rush into her apartment. We now had everyone's attention.

"If anyone moves or says a word, granny right here dies." I heard Max say.

I hoped they believed him. Max was a straight killer, and he would kill his own mother if she crossed him. We weren't in the business of murdering old ladies or kids, so I really did hope they played by our rules. Cam came rushing from the back of the apartment with a look of disappointment on his face.

"Where the fuck is Man?" Cam barked, flipping over the coffee table.

I looked over at the three frantic kids. Cam saw what I saw, then looked at JR and barked orders

"Yo, take them in one of them rooms in the back."

JR quickly gathered the kids and walked them toward the back of the apartment. Cam walked over to the couch and grabbed the boy who was sitting there by his shirt.

"Yo, when my brother catches y'all niggas, it's going to be a wrap." The boy yelled, trying to sound tough.

Cam turned his head and looked at the boy sideways. He made the wrong move by declaring he was Man's brother. That only meant one thing; collateral damage. Cam stepped away from the boy and looked at Max, who then raised his .45 and put a bullet in the middle of the boy's forehead. The elderly lady and another girl broke down and started screaming and hollering. We didn't pay that shit no mind. He took the life of one of ours, and that was the price.

We had to get low fast, because the neighbors definitely heard the shot, and we wasn't in any predicament to be dealing with the boys tonight. We had enough shit that needed to be handled.

"Yo bro, let's get low." I said as I walked to the back of the apartment to get JR.

As we stepped back into the living room, Cam had the chick by her throat.

"Tell that nigga Man that he's next!"

We back peddled out the apartment and down the stairs. We concealed our weapons as we weaved through the housing project, back to the car. We headed to one of our spots in Brownsville, and ended up staying there till the sun started to rise.

Skye

I squinted as my eyes tried to adjust to the sunlight that was beaming through my windows. I thought about last night, and reached over and took my phone off the nightstand. I was disappointed that I didn't have a call or text from Cameron. He just up and left the dinner last night without a word. I knew he was okay because his dad said he went to help Ty's dad, but he still could have called or texted me. Whatever though, I was not about to dwell on that. Aside from his little disappearing act last night, my parents had a good time. They clicked really well with his parents, which was a good thing.

I sat up in bed and looked around the room; I had decided to stay the night at my parent's house since I rode with them to Cameron's house. They didn't want me going home alone. As I looked around, memories flooded my thoughts. I missed home; I missed this room. I lost my virginity in here, and dealt with my first heart break in here. This was my sanctuary. I don't really know why I opted to move out last year, because I didn't have to. If it was up to my parents, they would have me living under their roof forever, but I wasn't with that.

I fell back onto the bed. I didn't have anything to do so I was going to take advantage of my opportunity to stay in bed. As I got comfortable, my phone started to vibrate, thinking it was Cameron, I answered without looking.

"Hello!" I yelled into the phone.

"Hey chica."

It was nice to hear from Ariana, but I wanted it to be Cameron so bad.

I masked my disappointment. "Hey girly, what you doing up this early?"

"Ty came over at like eight something this morning. He's in the shower now, though."

I was going to ask about Cameron, but the beeping on my other line interrupted me. I looked at the phone and saw his name flashing on my screen.

"Ari, this Cameron on my other line, let me call you right back girl." I hung up before she could respond.

"Now you know my number, Cameron!" I barked into the phone.

I was irate and planned on letting him know just how pissed off I was. He didn't speak and that pissed me off.

"Hello…"

I was ready to hang up, but he spoke up just in time.

"Where you at? Why you not home?"

What the hell? Was he questioning me like I was the one who disappeared for the night? I wanted to be mad, but something in his tone made me soften mine.

"I stayed at my parents. Are you there now?" I climbed out the bed and walked into the bathroom.

"Yeah, I need to see you." The sincerity in his voice made my heart melt.

"I'll call down to the front and have Jacob come up and let you in. I'll be there soon."

I ended the call and called Jacob. I knew it was totally against policy, but he was a friend, and would do a favor for me. As expected, he agreed to let him in.

****

When I got home, I found Cameron sitting on the couch, staring into space. When he finally realized I was there, he managed to show me his smile that I loved so much. I sat next to him and rested my head on his shoulder.

"I'm sorry I didn't call you, a lot went on last night. Rick was murdered."

I sat up and faced him; the look on his face was full of sorrow. I could see the pain he was trying to mask.

"I'm sorry for your loss baby, but I'm here for you if you want to talk, or if you need anything."

He kissed me and shook his head. "Nah, I'm straight. Don't want to talk about it at all."

That was what I didn't like about him. He felt he needed to be tough about everything and to everyone. He didn't have to be that way with me, but Cameron didn't understand that though.

"Okay, we don't have to talk about it."

I wasn't going to sit there in silence. I had on yesterday's clothes and wanted a shower badly. I got up and headed to my room, stopping at the hall closet to hang up my pea coat. Once I was in my room, I stripped and got in the shower. I was standing under the water, allowing the water to beat on my body. It felt amazing, reminding me how badly that I was in need of a spa trip. I suddenly felt air, so I turned around to find the shower glass pulled back, and Cameron standing there. I tried to hide my excitement, but I couldn't. I slowly looked down and had to gasp at the size of his dick.

"Can I join you?"

I smiled and stepped back, giving him space to step into the shower with me. I started to lather soap on my sponge, when I felt Cameron kiss my shoulder. I dropped the sponge and turned to face him. After a few seconds of looking into each other's eyes, out lips met. We kissed with fervor, and before I knew it, my back was against the shower wall. In one swift motion, he lifted me up and began to slide his rock hard manhood into my now dripping wet box.

"Damn, Skye you so tight ma."

As he inched in further, my body tensed up; he was big.

"Want me to stop? I don't want to hurt you."

It was nice that he cared, but hell no I didn't want him to stop.

I let out a soft "No," as he went deeper.

After a few strokes, the slight pain was erased and replaced with complete pleasure. I dug my nails into Cameron's back as I felt him hit my spot over and over.

"Cameronnnn" I moaned out his name as I felt a body shaking orgasm shoot through my body.

He put me down and turned me around, facing the wall. I was glad he was still holding me up, because my legs felt like jelly. As he entered me slowly from behind, I bit down on my lip and arched my back.

"Ya pussy feel mad good."

I wanted to yell duh, but I couldn't formulate any words; just moans, ooh's and ahh's. He slapped my ass, then gripped both cheeks as he pumped in and out. I felt another orgasm coming, and noticed his breathing got heavy and short, so I knew he was on the verge of busting. I threw my ass back and he pumped faster

"Shiiiiit!" Cameron called out as he bust his nut inside me.

I too released my juices all over his dick. I couldn't believe we just had sex without a condom. Don't get me wrong, the shit felt good, but that wasn't something I was into. I didn't want to ruin the moment, so instead, I said nothing. I simply picked up my sponge, washed, and got out the shower. I was in the middle of slipping on a t-shirt when Cameron came walking in the room with a towel wrapped around his waist. Damn, that nigga was fine. He walked over to where I was standing and kissed me. I felt a tingling between my legs but had no intentions on having sex with him again; not right now at least. I walked away as I put my wet hair up into a ponytail, using the hair tie I had on my wrist.

"Sk..." He called after me but his sentence was cut short by the ringing of his cell phone.

Thank goodness, because I wasn't trying to converse at the moment. I walked into the living room and flopped down on my couch. I knew I should have gone over some work, since class would be back in session in a few days. UGH! Thanksgiving break was entirely too short. I turned around because I heard footsteps approaching.

"I gotta go. I'll come back later or something."

Or something? Was that nigga serious? We had sex, and then he just decides to up and leave? I was not about to be one of them chicks who let a dude do whatever because he was cute, and had a good dick game. I'm good on that.

"Okay." I kept it short.

Cameron could go ahead with his little disappearing acts. At that point, I was feeling like Sweet Brown; ain't nobody got time for that! There were no more words shared between us. I heard his footsteps, then the front door closing. I decided not to dwell on the little situation with Cameron. I called up my girl Ariana to see what she was up to. She said Ty had just left, so we agreed to meet up for lunch and do some shopping.

Chapter Three

Ariana

When my taxi pulled up to Koi Restaurant, I stepped out into the brisk air. The cold and I never got along, so I put my Ralph Lauren riding boots to the pavement and quickly walked to the entrance of the restaurant. When I entered, I was greeted by a hostess. She was so polite, and that was another reason why I loved that place, besides the bomb ass sushi they served. Once I told her someone else would be joining me, she showed me to a nice intimate table for two. I removed my coat and got comfortable. I glanced at my No Label watch, wondering why Skye wasn't there yet. When I looked up, I saw the hostess leading her over to where I was. I smiled as I stood up and hugged my best friend. Skye was my girl, we been friends since birth basically. Our fathers are fraternity brothers, so our families are extremely close. I felt a little bad that we hadn't really been hanging out lately. Between my job at the radio station, and spending time with Ty, I rarely had time for anything. I figured since she'd been kicking it heavy with Cam, the time apart didn't bother her.

"Girl!" Skye yelled, as she got comfortable in her seat.

I knew she had some tea.

"Yes, hunny." I chuckled as I picked up the menu and scanned it.

"This boy is driving me crazy."

Suddenly, she had my undivided attention. I hadn't had a clue that there was trouble in paradise. Yea, it had been too long since I've kicked it with my right hand.

"What's going on? I thought things were going well."

I was confused. Skye sighed and began to give me the run down.

"Things were; well, I guess they are going well. I just get the feeling like he's keeping something from me. Cameron keeps playing these disappearing acts, and the shit is getting old quick!"

She was frustrated. I could tell so I let her get everything off her chest.

"I feel like maybe he has a girl, and if he does that's cool, but keep it real with me. I would be pissed because we had sex, but I would definitely get over it. You know me, I can deal with a lot, but being lied is not something I am fond of."

Wait did this chick just said they had sex? She had to be really feeling dude, because Skye was definitely one of those ninety day rule chicks that Steve Harvey talked about in *Think Like A Man.*

I took a sip of the water that the waitress just placed on the table, before speaking. "Chica, I know that can be frustrating, but I also know that you cannot speculate on what Cam is keeping from you, if he's keeping anything at all. The best way to find out what is what, is to flat out ask him."

The look Skye gave me told me that she agreed with what I said. It was true; the quickest way to lose a nigga is to accuse him of shit he not doing. I didn't want my girl to go down that road.

"You're right, but enough about the Cameron and Skye soap opera. How are things with my day one?"

We placed our orders before I began to give Skye my spiel about how things were between me and Ty. Man, I had to admit, I was really feeling him. He was considerate, real, and his dick game was one hundred. I could definitely see us on some long term shit, and he expressed to me that he felt the same. No I wasn't in love, but I was heavily in like. Yea, that's how I would put it. Skye listened attentively as I ran down all that had been going on, and of course she offered her advice. Once our food arrived, the talking ceased. We were in shape, but we loved us some food.

****

Lunch was great, but it was time to tear up the shops on Fifth Avenue. Catching a taxi was easy since hundreds of them filled the streets of NYC at all hours of the day. Once we hit Fifth Avenue, we hit all our favorite spots; Bergdorf Goodman, M.A.C, Gucci, Christian Louboutin, and heap of others. Shopping with my girl was always an all-day thing, which is why I didn't head home till about 8:00pm.

****

As I walked through the door of my Condo, I felt my cell phone vibrate. I dropped my bags on the living room floor and grabbed it out my purse. I smiled when I saw Ty's name, and answered.

"Wassup handsome?"

I may have sounded a bit to chipper but whatever; I didn't mind my man knowing he was missed.

"What you doing?"

I sat on the couch, holding the phone between my shoulder and ear as I took off my boots. "I just got home babe, I went to eat and shopping with Skye."

His background was noisy as hell. I almost wanted to tell him to call me back, but I decided against that.

"Pack a bag. We gotta run to Atlanta, and we just gonna stay there and kick it till Sunday."

Did he just say run to Atlanta like it's the next borough or something?

"What you going to Atlanta for babe?"

I didn't really need to ask that because I was going. A weekend in the A sounded good to me.

"Just to chill and shit. You coming?"

Shit, he definitely didn't need to ask me twice. "Yea baby I'll go. Imma pack now. Are you on your way to get me?"

Ty yelled at someone in the background to turn the music down, before shifting back to our conversation. "Yea, be ready in an hour."

After getting off the phone with my babe, I gathered all my bags and headed to my room to figure out what I would be taking for my weekend trip and pack. I walked back and forth between my closet and the dresser, grabbing everything I thought I would need for a night. Once I had out about a week's worth of things I sorted through it all and narrowed it down. I had a bad habit of over packing but I was trying hard to keep it simple for once. I decided on a few outfits, and shockingly only two pairs of shoes. If for some reason I needed something else, I could also hit up Lenox mall or something. Who was I kidding? I was going to hit up Lenox anyway; it was a ritual whenever I was in the A.

I was in the middle of putting my boots back on when my cellphone started ringing. I grabbed it off the night stand and answered; it was Ty letting me know that he was downstairs. I was excited to be going away with him for the weekend. I didn't want to waste any more time, so I put on my coat and grabbed my duffel bag. I needed to let my parents know I would be away for the weekend, so I texted my mom while I was in the elevator, letting her know that I would be with Ty.

When I got outside, I saw Ty standing outside of a black Range Rover and I headed over to him. Damn my man looked good. He reminded me of the singer Tyrese. I was totally into dark chocolate, so Ty was just my speed. I stood on my tip toes and kissed him, before sliding in the back of the Range.

"Hey Cam."

"Hmm... if Cam was coming, why wasn't Skye invited?" I thought to myself.

I thought back to the conversation I had with her earlier, and figured something definitely was up.

"Wassup Ari, I don't think you met this nigga, but this our boy Jr."

I said wassup to their friend before grabbing my phone and texting Skye.

Wassup Chica, Ty invited me to go to Atlanta till Sunday with him, and Cameron going too. I'm definitely going to find out what's going on with this dude. No worries, I got you.

I slipped my phone back in my purse before getting comfortable and laying my head on Ty's shoulder as we started our Journey to the airport.

Chapter Four

Cameron

I turned on my phone as soon as we exited the airport. I looked through my text messages to make sure I didn't get an important message. I saw Skye texted me, so I opened hers first.

Honestly Cameron I'm good on your bullshit. Really? A trip that my bestfriend was invited on but I wasn't? I'm not even tripping on the fact that you didn't invite me. The fact that I wasn't important enough to tell that you were going out of town is what bothers me. Especially after you dipped from my house right after fucking me. But it's cool. Like I said, I'm good on it. Enjoy your time in Atlanta, and don't think to hit me up when your back home either.

I felt bad for not inviting Skye to Atlanta but this wasn't a social trip for me, it was business. Ty had me tight; I didn't understand why he had to invite Ariana, but I couldn't really be mad. He was doing enough by keeping our business dealings under wraps because I didn't want it to get back to Skye. I really needed to make some decisions about that girl if I wanted her in my life. I would definitely have to put her on game soon.

My thoughts were interrupted by Ty tapping me to get my attention.

"What happened?" I asked turning around to face him.

"Our ride here."

I followed him and Ariana over to where our home boy Matt was waiting for us in his truck. Matt been our boy for a while, we met him back in seventh grade when he first moved to Brooklyn. We lost touch right before we went to high school because his grandmother got sick, and he and his moms had to come down to the A to take care of her and shit. I was kind of surprised when he reached out. He was going through a tough time and needed some homies to lean on. I was never in the business of letting my homies starve, and I wasn't going to start with Matt. I set him up with a team and some weight, and he was eating good because of it.

I climbed in the passenger seat to give the love birds some space in the backseat.

"What up boy?" I said, bumping fists with Matt.

"Same shit different day man."

I nodded at his nonchalant response, as he pulled off. I sat back and stared out the window as we rode through the streets of Atlanta.

Although I wanted to call Skye and apologize for not keeping her in the loop, I couldn't. That trip was important; we were sent there so that I could meet with our connect Miguel Alvarez. Miguel was the current Mexican drug lord of the notorious cartel Los Jefes. They were ruthless and known for their involvement in human trafficking, gun trafficking, racketeering, and supplying niggas like my pops with the purest white girl known to man. My father had been dealing with those niggas for as far back as I could remember; since Miguel's father, Ricardo was boss. So it's pretty safe to say things should have gone smooth, because our track record with them had been nothing short of impeccable. However, fucking with those crazy Mexicans, you don't really know what to expect so I had to be on point. After the loss we had taken during the hit on our warehouse, who knew how this meeting would play out. It was their money that was taken. I wasn't too worried about that though, because we weren't no crab ass dudes who came with a boat load of excuses. We came ready to pay back every cent that was lost.

****

When we got to the hotel, all I wanted to do was shower and hit the bed. It was a little past two in the morning. Usually I was a night owl, but since the shit with Rick went down, I just felt drained. Don't get me wrong, losing homies really came with the territory, but it was fucked up but this was my reality. It's just that Rick wasn't just a homie; he was as close to an uncle as I had since both my parents were the only children. Losing him really took a toll on me. Not to mention that I had to see his wife and kids soon. How the fuck was I supposed to face them?

After the shower, I wasn't in the mood for nothing. I climbed in the bed butt ass naked; a nigga just wanted to relax. I laid there awake for a minute, thinking about Skye, wishing she was next to me until I succumbed to sleep.

****

The next morning, I was awakened by the sound of someone banging on my room door. I sucked my teeth, and climbed out the bed. I totally forgot that I slept in my birthday suit, but that shit felt good though. I walked over to where I left my duffel, and rummaged through it, looking for something to throw on. I pulled out a pair of Ralph Lauren sweats and threw them on, before walking over to the door.

I looked through the peep-hole, and saw that it was that nigga Ty.

"Why the fuck you banging on the door like you them boys, bro?" I barked with aggravation seeping through my tone, as I opened the door.

If anyone knew that shit annoyed me, it should have been him. We slapped fives and bump shoulders before he walked through the door.

"Son, why you not ready? You know the meeting at twelve, right?"

I looked at the Presidential Rolex that I had on my wrist, checking the time. It was already 10:45.

"Fuck, I told myself to set my alarm and shit last night, but a nigga was beat."

I grabbed my duffel and flopped down on the bed to pick out an outfit. When it came to my clothes, I was an indecisive ass nigga. All my shit was fly, but it didn't matter. I had to love the fit or I wouldn't feel right. Too bad I didn't have the time to be picky. I settled for a Balmain shirt, hoodie, and a pair of Nudie Jeans. I got off the bed and headed into the bathroom, leaving Ty to whatever he was doing in his phone.

Even though I showered before I went to bed, I was a morning shower type of nigga, so I brushed my teeth and jumped in. That shit felt good, but I knew I was working on borrowed time so I had to make it quick. When I got out, I dried off and got dressed. When I walked back into the room, Ty was on the balcony smoking. As bad as I wanted to get high, I made it my business to go into all meetings sober; especially fucking with these crazy ass Mexicans. I tapped on the balcony door and signaled for Ty to come on.

"Yo, did you get a burner from Matt?"

I prayed he remembered, because although I couldn't go into the meeting with a piece, I felt much better know my nigga was packing and waiting out front need be.

"Yea, he dropped the shit off this morning and left me keys to one of his whips for us to use."

I should have known; my nigga was always on his shit. As we waited for the elevator, I remembered he had Ari out there.

"Where you told shorty you was going?" I asked him as we stepped onto the elevator.

"I told her I was going to the gym with you, and left her some money to go shopping."

I laughed because that nigga was a clown. "The gym though, bro?"

Ty knew it was a dumb ass lie so he joined me in laughter. "It worked, so fuck it."

I nodded my head because he was right. Once we got outside, we walked around the block to the parking lot where Matt had parked his car. When I saw the shit he left for us I had to shake my head. Out of all cars, that nigga left us with a Prius. Did we look like Prius driving cats? Ty must have been thinking the same thing, because we looked at each other and bust out laughing.

"A Prius son? Nigga could have left us the truck." I said as I climbed in the passenger seat.

I couldn't really complain though, because Matt provided us with wheels to handle our business. We had to be thankful for that.

****

When we pulled up to the little Mexican spot on Piedmont Road, I mentally prepared myself to deal with whatever bullshit they were going to throw at me. I looked over at Ty, and no words needed to be shared. I knew that nigga would never let anything happen to me if he could help it, so I wasn't even worried. I slapped fives with my brother and hopped out the car.

As I entered the restaurant, I took in the scenery just to make sure nothing seemed out of the ordinary. I made this trip often enough to know what was routine and what wasn't. I spotted the owner's daughter, Lisa; she was bad as fuck. I was never into dating outside my race, but I made an exception for this half Mexican half black chick. I wouldn't really call what we had dating though. She was rocking skin tight jeans that hugged her fat ass, which made me stare a little. When she saw me she smiled and walked over to me.

"Hola, Stranger." She playfully slapped my arm.

That was her *I missed the dick* gesture. Yea, I smashed shorty on every trip I took to the A, and as bad as I wanted this trip to be the same as the others, I had a shorty at home.

"Wassup, can you tell Miguel I'm here?"

She looked at me confused. I knew she was expecting me to flirt and shit, but I wanted to really see where things could go with Skye, so I was going to try the monogamous thing.

"Oh I see, just business this trip, huh?"

I nodded and she turned away to let them know I was here. I tried to help it, but I couldn't help it as I watched her ass with every stride she took. I waited a few minutes before Aurelio appeared in the doorway of the back room, signaling me to come. I headed in his direction, avoiding eye contact with Lisa. Once I reached the door he was standing at, we shook hands and he moved over so I could enter the room. As usual, six heavily armed Mexicans were standing there while Aurelio searched me. Once he saw I was clean, he nodded, giving the guards the okay to let me pass. As I walked further into the room, I spotted Miguel sitting down with two chicks eating. He must have felt my presence because he looked up from his food and smiled.

"Young Cam. How are you today?"

I hated when he called me young Cam. I was a grown ass man, but of course I had to bite my tongue and suppress the annoyance I had from being called that dumb shit. He stood up to shake my hand and signaled for me to sit.

"Wassup Miguel, I'm cool. How are you?"

He sighed and shook his head; I already knew where this was going. "I was doing pretty well my friend. That is until I got a phone call about your spot being hit and me losing five hundred thousand dollars. You could understand why I would be in a not so great mood right?"

Miguel stared at me and waited for me to respond, I was just making sure he spoke his piece before I said mine, because I knew those Mexicans wouldn't hesitate to shoot if they felt I disrespected their boss. I knew that because it's exactly what any nigga on my team would do if my father was disrespected.

"Miguel, I understand your frustrations but you have nothing to worry about."

His eyebrows went up, that nigga wanted to raise his own damn blood pressure because nothing I said should have put him on edge.

"So you telling me that I should not be concerned when it comes to my money?"

If Miguel would have just shut the fuck up and let me finish what I was saying he would have known the answer to that dumb ass question.

"Yea, my father didn't ask for this meeting for me to come at you with excuses as to why the money gone. There was a problem I'm here with the solution. You weren't due to get paid for another week, but I'm prepared to pay you back what is owed with interest for the hassle, NOW!"

I had to say now hard so he would understand I wasn't there on some bull shit.

"I see why my father had no issues dealing with your father for so many years; I appreciate the way you guys do business. How much interest are we talking about here?"

I sat up straight and looked him directly in his eyes. I wanted Miguel to see how serious I was. My eyes dared him to try and play me for some rookie as nigga, as my next statement fell from my lips.

"Name your price, Miguel."

The ultimate test, it was a win, win situation for him. He was getting what he was owed a week early with extra. I wasn't one to be played for a fool, because I wasn't new to that shit. Miguel sat back and pondered over my statement, I could tell he was battling with taking me to the bank, or doing the right thing and keeping shit civil. When money was involved, niggas tended to get greedy. I hoped for everyone's sake that Miguel wouldn't go there. He clasped his hands together and leaned forward.

"I like y'all, Cam. The numbers we pull in monthly dealing with your father are astronomical. With that being said, I'll just take what is owed."

Was that man testing me? Why couldn't we just handle shit straight up? What was with the mind games?

"Nah, on behalf of my pops and our organization, we feel it's only right to give you a bit extra. How's $750,000?"

I went in with the intentions on giving those niggas a whole extra $500,000 but since he wanted play mind games that got cut in half. Miguel smirked, I knew that nigga was fishing, but I wasn't about to bite the bait.

"$750,000 sounds good, I hope you didn't travel with that type of cash."

I didn't like being underestimated. Who the fuck would travel on a plane with $750,000 in dirty money? Not anyone with a fucking brain. That nigga annoyed me, and I was glad that meeting was over. We discussed plans for the money transaction to take place back in NY in the next few days, and I dipped.

Chapter Five

Ty

When I saw Cam coming out the restaurant, I let out a heavy breath because you just never knew when dealing with those Mexicans. To say those dudes were crazy would be an understatement. I started up the car as Cam got in, and pulled off. I glanced at him, and could tell he had some shit on his mind.

"How'd it go, bro?"

He shook his head side to side and rubbed his temple. "Man, it went cool but dealing with them cats is a headache. Everything is a fucking mind game, or a test."

I could honestly say that was part of the job description I was glad I didn't have to deal with. I didn't trust the Mexicans at all, but our supply was basically endless with grade A shit, so I couldn't really complain.

"What you trying to get into the rest of the time we out here?"

I had a few things on my mind, with fucking the shit out of Ariana at the top of the list.

"Bro you can just drop me off at the hotel. I brought the books a nigga need to get in some studying. Back to school Monday, I and I haven't picked up a book the entire vacation."

I respected that; I mean how could I not? My nigga was waist deep is this business, but still managed to keep school first. I wish I had the will power to do the same, but school wasn't my thing. I was done with the school shit after high school.

"Aight bro."

The rest of the ride was silent, aside from the hip hop that blasted through the car stereo system. I wasn't really feeling this music though; not a big fan of down South rap. 2 Chainz was my hitter, but I had to listen to that nigga's music in moderation because I got tired of that shit after a while. When we pulled up to the hotel, Cam and I gave each other dap and he got out. I wondered if Ariana was still in the room, so I pulled out my phone and called her.

"Hey baby." She answered on the first ring.

I loved that she always was happy to hear from me.

"What's good love? You still in the room?" I heard some nigga trying to get her attention and got a mad. "Yo!" I barked into the phone.

"Yea baby, my bad. This nigga pulled my arm trying to get my attention, and I had to check his ass. But nah, I'm at Lenox. You meeting up with me, or you still with Cam?"

That nigga better be glad I wasn't in the vicinity. "Yea, I'm on my way."

****

When I pulled into Lenox Mall parking area, I drove around for about 15 minutes trying to find parking. I was relieved when I saw a blue Honda pulling out of a spot. I quickly swerved into it before anyone else can snatch it. As I walked toward one of the entrances, I texted Ari to see where she was. She replied telling me to meet her at the Louis Vuitton store. I hadn't been to this mall in a minute, so I had to grab one of them brochures with the map on it to find the store.

Ariana

When I saw my man walking into the store, I smiled. I couldn't believe how totally smitten I was by him. Ty was everything I could want in a dude. He had time for himself, and managed to have time for me. He was clear about his feelings and where we stood with each. I didn't ask for much; just a loyal nigga with good dick. Ty gave me that, so your girl didn't have any complaints.

He walked over to me as I was looking at the pocketbooks through the glass case, and stood directly behind me, kissing my neck. I felt my panties moisten. Why did his touch have that effect on me? I turned to face him, and playfully bit his lip.

"I missed you too." I said as I turned away to look at the bags again.

I couldn't decide between the Deesse GM, and the Navy Blue Alma GM. After a few minutes of debating I decided on the Alma. The navy would go fine with a pair of jeans on a regular day. After paying for the bag, Ty and I walked hand in hand throughout the mall, stopping at stores we liked on the way. After a few hours of tearing up the mall, we stopped for food and were ready to retire to the hotel. I was so happy his friend let him borrow a car, because getting a taxi was hell for me. I had to remember this wasn't New York.

As Ty put the bags in the back seat, I got in the car and decided to call Skye. She had to be bored out her mind. I mean we had tons of friends, but when it came to kicking it and going out it was just us two. So I know with me out of town, my girl was in her crib drowning in them textbooks. The phone rang four times, and I was ready to hang up when she finally answered.

"Hey bestie."

Eww she needed to clear her throat sounding like a sick little boy.

"Yuck trick, clear your throat." I said laughing at her.

Skye laughed with me. "Shut up, I was knocked out. But thanks for calling me. I need to get up and get some studying done."

See, I knew it. School, sleep, and no play; her lifelong ritual.

"Oh, I was just calling to see what you were up to. Ty and I are on our way back to the hotel. We went shopping at Lenox."

I was waiting for her to….

"Tell Ty I said hey, and where's Cameron?"

I laughed to myself. She interrupted my thoughts, but that's what I was waiting for. I knew Skye better than she knew herself sometimes.

"Ty, she said hey, and where's Cam?" I turned to him waiting for his response.

"Wassup, Skye, and he at the hotel. He said he needed to study."

I didn't need to repeat that because I held the phone so she could hear. I put the phone back to my ear as she started to talk.

"Oh, okay. Well thank you for checking on me doll. Enjoy your time there, and call me when you touch home."

We said our goodbyes and ended the call.

****

When we got back to our hotel room my, intentions were to fuck my nigga brains out till we went to bed, but there were some things I needed to discuss with him. While he was on the balcony, I jumped in the shower, using that time to get my thoughts together. My approach needed to be correct if I had any chance of getting the answers that I wanted. I washed and thought hard. When I stepped out the shower, I put on my robe and tied it as I walked into the room. He was looking extremely good, sitting on the edge of the bed in nothing but boxer briefs and socks. I sat next to him and rubbed his shoulders. I wanted him relaxed for when my questions started pouring out. Ty looked up at me and smiled.

"Why you didn't get me so I could shower with you?"

Shit, I didn't even think about that.

"I didn't want to bother you baby, plus you will have plenty more opportunities to shower with me."

He nodded his head in agreement and said "True."

Alright Ariana this your chance. I had to be my own cheerleader.

"Baby, wassup with Cam?"

The look he gave me almost made me regret that I asked. I should have figured out a better way to start the conversation, but I wasn't about to turn back now. I told my girl I would get to the bottom of this shit for her, and that's what I planned to do.

"What you mean?" He asked me.

I decided to just put it all out there; I wasn't about that beating around the bush life.

"Look baby, I know that it's not really any of our business what goes on between them, but Skye is my best friend. Nah, that's my sister, and her best interest is always first to me. She feels like Cam not really feeling her or he's keeping something from her."

I paused to give him a chance to speak but he said nothing, I could see that Ty was listening, but decided to stay mute. That was fine; I wasn't going to stop.

"I just feel like if he isn't feeling her, he needs to just be honest with her, instead of stringing her along. We're grown right? She's tired of him dipping on her without any explanation. Shit, I would be tired too. As females, we don't expect y'all to give us a complete run down of your daily agenda, but be considerate. For example, Cam out here in Atlanta; you invited me, but he couldn't invite Skye? Put not inviting her aside, he didn't even tell her he was going out of town, and that's beyond fucked up. Skye isn't an ugly weak broad, so she don't need to put all her chips on a nigga who don't want her."

Finally he spoke up; I was honestly running out of shit to say.

"It's not even like that."

Wow, was he serious? After everything I said he replied with that bullshit?

Nah, that wasn't going to cut it.

"So what is it like?"

Ty sighed, giving me all the answers I wanted plus more. He revealed to me that he and Cam were both major players in an illegal operation ran by Cam's dad. He spared me the details, which I was thankful for, because I didn't have time to be an accessory to anyone's bull. I was shocked though; Cam had my girl over there thinking he was some law abiding citizen going to law school and shit, when the whole time he was living this other life. It explained the disappearing acts, but it didn't explain the dishonesty. Skye could forgive a lot, but lying wasn't one of the things on that list. I, on the other hand, was much more understanding. Living that life wasn't really something you just flat out tell people. However, if you have intentions on dealing with someone on a serious level, some information needed to be shared. I never asked Ty what he did for a living because quite honestly, it didn't matter to me. I mean, I saw that he was able to provide for himself, so I knew he wasn't a broke nigga. Plus, he wouldn't be the first hustler I dated, and if things didn't work out, he wouldn't be the last.

When he was done telling me everything, I promised I wouldn't tell Skye, but I was only giving Cameron till Tuesday to come clean. Keeping secrets wasn't something I felt comfortable with when it came to Skye because we shared everything, but that was something that was truly Cam's place to share. After that conversation, a girl was beat. I had plans on putting Ty to bed, but was no longer in the mood, which was why when he headed in the bathroom, I got comfortable and dozed off.

Cameron

Damn, I couldn't fall asleep for shit. I'd been laying there, tossing and turning for like an hour. Skye crossed my mind as my phone vibrated, and I low key hoped it was her. It wasn't though; just a text from Ty.

Yo bro, it's about time you have that conversation with ol girl if you serious about her. Ari pressed me about how she feels you dissing her and shit. If shorty worth you being with her, she gonna ride. If she not, she'll dip and that would be doing you a favor. So just let her know fam. I'm going to bed though. Nigga don't over sleep and make us miss the flight.

As much as I didn't want to admit it, Ty was right. I wasn't saying I wanted to marry shorty or nothing like that, but I did want to be with her. If Skye wanted to be with me, she was going to understand, and if she didn't, it was whatever. Chicks come and go so that's something I would never stress about. It didn't change the fact that I wanted it to be her though. I knew what I had to do. I scrolled through the phone book on my phone till I found her name. I contemplated on calling her, but opted out and decided to just text her.

Wassup beautiful? You probably sleep and shit, so I hope this don't wake you up. But I just wanted to apologize about how I been handling shit lately. I wanna see you tomorrow and talk to you. If you with that, come pick me up from JFK. Our flight gets in at 2:00pm. If you not there, I'll know what it is. Goodnight ma, sleep tight.

Something told me Skye would be there. The feeling that came over me made me smile. I was still trying to figure out what it was about shorty that had me ready to break all the rules and let her in. That's the last thing I thought about before I fell asleep.

Chapter Six

Skye

I hated the fact that I couldn't sleep when the sun was shining in my room. For some reason, I kept forgetting to close my blinds before I went to bed. I looked at the time; it was only 9 o'clock in the morning. It was Sunday and I had absolutely nothing to do.

"Thank you Mr. Sun!" I said out loud to no one.

I let out a huge sigh before grabbing my phone. My morning ritual was to check missed calls and text messages as soon as I got up. Although I was pissed, I still smiled as I read the text message from Cameron. He wanted me to pick him up from the airport at 2:00 so we could talk. I don't know if it was curiosity or me just genuinely wanting to see him; maybe a bit of both. Regardless of the reason, I formulated in my brain that I was going to pick him up for sure. I sat my phone down and headed to the bathroom to brush my teeth and shower. While I was in the shower, I decided to sing Olivia's "Walk away." I knew I had a voice that only a mother would cheer on, which is why I was singing in the shower with no one else around. I laughed out loud, thinking about what anyone would say if they heard me singing.

After my shower, I dried off and headed to the kitchen to find some food, naked. I was comfortable in my skin, plus I was home alone, so who did I need to cover up for? I searched through the refrigerator for something that was already cooked, because I didn't feel like making anything. I spotted a salad that I had from yesterday and did my happy dance; which was similar to Michael Jackson's moon walk. I grabbed the salad and a bottle of water before sitting down at the island and getting my grub on.

Man, that salad hit every spot possible. I must have been really hungry because that salad tasted like a full course meal. My tummy was satisfied and it was time to *get my life* as Tamar Braxton liked to say. I headed back to my bedroom and fixed the bed before heading into my walk in closet. I searched through the racks that held my jeans and settled for a pair of black Burberry jeans.

"Simple enough," I thought to myself.

I shifted a handful of hangers to the other side, and the first shirt I laid eyes on was a black Burberry sweater.

"Today is going to be a good day." I said out loud.

It was rare that I was ever able to decide on an outfit that fast. Maybe because I wasn't trying to be extremely fancy, since I was only going to pick up ol boy from the airport. I applied lotion to my skin before putting on my panties and bra, and then got dressed. I needed something to do to waste time since their flight wouldn't be getting in until 2:00. I glanced at my textbook and sighed; might as well get some studying done since I had free time.

****

I arrived at the airport at twenty minutes until two. I expected there to be way more traffic than it was. It's cool though, and I sent Cameron a text letting him know where I was parked, and sat back and listened to music. A little bit after two, I saw Ariana, Cameron, and Ty headed towards my car. I had to admit, I got a little bit happy seeing him. I missed him, even though I didn't want to admit it. When they got close, I hit the button on my door that unlocked the other doors so they could hop in. As soon as Cameron was seated, he leaned over and kissed me. I wasn't surprised, but what did surprise me was the fact that I didn't pull away. I wanted to be mad at him, but my mind wouldn't let me.

"Hey guys, Ty where am I taking you?" I turned around and waited for him to answer.

The look he gave me said I should already know the answer.

"Never mind, Arianna house it is."

We all laughed as I pulled off.

****

After dropping Ariana and Ty off, Cameron and I grabbed some food from Amy Ruth's uptown, and headed to my place. I was really anxious to know what he wanted to talk about. It better have been good because at that point, I was ready to chalk whatever we had going on up, and leave it at friends; or just don't deal with each other at all. At least that's what I was trying to make myself believe.

When we got in the house, we wasted no time. We headed straight to the kitchen, washed our hands, and started on our food. I guess that salad wasn't the full course meal I imagined it to be, because in my head I was singing 'R.I.P I'm about to kill this food' in my best young Jeezy voice. That made me chuckle to myself.

"What you smiling about?"

Oops, he saw me.

"Nothing, but wassup?" I asked as I scooped up spoonful of rice.

"I don't really want to ruin the moment right now."

Cameron didn't even bother looking up at me while he was talking. That's that bullshit; what was he hiding? A chick? A baby? Was he gay? All of the above? What the fuck? Now my mind was racing a mile a minute, and I was trying to catch up with it so I could formulate what I needed to say next.

"Cameron!"

I didn't shout, but I said his name as stern as I possibly could, because he needed to hear and understand the seriousness in my tone. I guess he heard it because he finally had the balls to look me in my face.

"Say whatever it is that you need to say."

He sighed, dropping his shoulders a little bit. I mean damn what could be so bad? He acting like he was about to tell me he killed my puppy or some shit.

"Aight, Skye look, this is not easy for me. I never felt like I wanted to have the type of relationship with a female, where I would need to tell her the shit I'm about to tell you."

Cameron paused, I hoped he wasn't waiting for me to respond, because I had nothing to say until he got whatever it is off his chest.

"I'm really feeling you. I mean, I'm sure you know that but at the same time I haven't really been doing my best to show you that. I want to though."

That nigga could really beat around the bush. To say I was uninterested in the pre-pep talk would be being nice. Like get to the point already.

"I haven't been completely honest with you, but I haven't been dishonest either. I would just say that I been omitting information."

I could never have prepared myself for what Cameron said to me next. Like really dude? A drug dealer, or supplier, whatever his position was in the whole thing? That's not something you keep from your girl. I don't know if it was just me, but I would want to know if it was a possibility that a nigga would kidnap me or worse, just because of my association with you. Don't get me wrong, I'm not one to judge; I say get it how you live by all means, but just keep it real with me. To think that this nigga was preaching *that I'm a real nigga, I'm a different breed* shit. Nah bro, you the same. What do I even say to that shit? Part of me wanted to kick the nigga out, but part of me wanted to be there; to be with him. I was built to handle that, I knew that for sure. My only worry was would it be worth it.

"Can you say something? Anything, even if you just wanna yell."

Hearing his voice turned me away from the rant that was taking place in the back of my mind.

"Cameron, what do you want me to say?"

If he wanted to hear me say it was okay, I wouldn't hold my breath if I was him, because this shit wasn't okay in the least bit.

"Anything, Skye."

I looked him in the eyes, which I should not have done. Seeing how sincere Cameron could be when talking to me always made me weak, and forget why I was ever mad. Unfortunately for him, it wouldn't be that easy this time.

"I mean, it is what is. How do you manage? I mean you really living a double life. To think, I thought this shit only happened in movies. Let me be clear though, I'm not mad because of the things you're involved in, Cameron. I'm mad because you didn't keep it real with me. I mean, I understand that some things you're not at liberty to discuss with me, but to just keep me totally in the dark? That wasn't fair. It's been almost four months that we been kicking it,

Cameron, and I was always honest and upfront with you. Why couldn't you be the same way with me?"

That was a rhetorical question, because I didn't want to hear his excuses. I was happy that guy was smart, because he didn't even fix his lips to give me any.

"I'm ready. I'm willing to tell you whatever you want to know. I want us to work, Skye. I really want to see where this could go."

I couldn't deny the fact that I wanted the same thing. I would only be lying to myself, so I listened.

Chapter Seven

Matt

I was glad those niggas were out of my city. I almost couldn't control the urge to kill them the minute I picked them up from the airport. I would have fucked the bitch first; she was cute. Ultimately, I would have had to kill her ass too though. I couldn't stand that nigga Cam. I don't give a fuck if he my brother or not, it ain't like he knows he is. Our bitch ass father Hassan kept me a secret because he already had his little man. Ty, on the other hand was collateral damage; he had to get it just because he was so close to Cam. It was fucked up because he was actually a cool dude. Oh well though, it's just the way the cookie crumbled.

I sat back smoking my blunt, and listening to music. I was in my zone. Shit was coming together nicely. It's fucked up that shit had to go this way, but desperate times called for desperate measures. I remembered the shit like it was yesterday man. I was in like 7th grade or some shit, and my mom's had lost her job; shit was rough. It had always been me and her. I never met my dad, and as far as I was concerned the nigga was dead. So when my mother told me we were moving to New York so that my dad could help us out and shit, I was shocked. I was mad at first because he wasn't there all them years, but at the same time it felt good, like I was finally getting the piece of me back that was missing. I was a naïve ass little nigga.

When we got to New York, one of my grandmother's friends had got us a room in a shelter. A FUCKING SHELTER! At that time I didn't feel anyway about it, because like I said, we were in a fucked up place. So, I was thankful just to have a roof over my head. All that changed on the day I met my father, though. He rolled up to the park that he met me and my mother at, in a decked out ass Benz. The nigga had security and shit, so I knew he had to be that nigga out here. I was young, but I grew up in the Bluff; one of the most dangerous places in Atlanta. To say my hood had a high crime rate would be putting it lightly. I was on game from a young'n, so his swag and demeanor told me what he was about before he even opened his mouth.

Here I was a little nigga, getting a little hype that my pops was somebody, and not just some weak ass dude; until he said the words that changed my life forever.

"What the fuck you call me for? Why did you even come back to NY?"

Just reliving the moment made me cringe. I remember them arguing back and forth for a good thirty minutes and not once during that time did he acknowledge me. He tossed my mother a hundred dollar bill and bounced.

That was the last time I saw or even spoke to him for a while. She had finally got this waitressing job, and we were able to afford a decent place. It wasn't in the best area and she wanted me to have a fighting chance, so she sent me to school across town. That's where I met Cam and Ty. I was a bum nigga; couldn't make friends for shit, and chicks didn't wanna be bothered. The ones who did, only spoke because they felt bad for me. One day, Cam and Ty rolled up on me in the locker room before gym and gave me two duffel bags full with brand new gear; fly shit too. From that moment on, we hung tough. I had no idea that Cam was my brother, although I looked at him as such because of the way he and Ty held me down.

It wasn't until we graduated that I found out who he was. After he crossed the stage receiving his diploma, I watched him run to his family. There was my bitch ass sperm donor. I didn't say anything though, until I got home that night and told my mother. That's when she finally told me the whole story about her and my dad. She was one of his workers; took trips up and down the 95 transporting drugs and money. One night they were drunk and fucked, and nine months later, there I was. My mother knew he had a wife and she had given birth to her son just a few months prior, so she didn't want to stir up any beef. My mother wasn't the confrontational type. She reached out to my pops, who gave her fifty thousand dollars and told her to bounce. She felt it wouldn't be smart to go against him, so she left and never looked back.

It was summer time, and I would be in high school come fall. I heard rumors around how Cam and Ty were doing little jobs for our pops and shit, so I felt like he should let me get down. I mean, I was entitled to everything Cam was entitled to, only difference was I didn't want shit for free. I didn't even want to be acknowledged as his son; just a little job to keep myself fly and entertain my lady friends. I had to be patient though, because I couldn't just run up to him at any given time. Luckily for me, Cam and I ended up playing in the same summer league, and I caught up with our pops after one of the games. That nigga gave me one hundred dollars and told me to go cop the new Jordan's.

At that moment, the resentment I had for him exploded. I didn't know how to control my anger so I started acting out. I linked with some niggas I met in Cypress and started getting into all type of shit. That's when my grandmother got sick, and I had to move back to Atlanta. I kept in touch with my Cypress niggas though; that's how I found out they were beefing with Cam and his team. My nigga Man and them had the upper hand because they had an inside man. Shit, sounded like an easy come up for me. All my ill feelings resurfaced, and of course I agreed to get down. You hear people preach that woman scorned shit; but what about a little boy, neglected and rejected by his own father? Fuck being scorned, I was out for blood!

Chapter Eight

Skye

Since the heart to heart Cameron and I had the other night, things had been great. I really didn't have any complaints. Other than the few nights after Rick's funeral, he made more time for me, and made it his business to have breakfast and dinner with me every single day. Most people would probably say we were moving extremely fast, but good thing we weren't most people. We were grown, and knew what we wanted. I didn't see a problem with that. We were becoming closer and closer by the minute. He did a complete 360 in terms of being honest and not disappearing. The lines of communication for us were open and clear. When he was in the street he even checked in, on some *"Baby just letting you know I'm safe"* type shit. Oh, let's not forget, the sex was immaculate.

I sat up in the bed and looked over at Cameron; he was sleeping peacefully, but wouldn't be for long though. I made a mental note to thank him for being a back sleeper. It made what I had plans for much easier. I pulled the covers back, slid off my Victoria Secret thong and straddled him. He didn't budge... Damn, he could sleep through anything. I didn't feel defeated yet. I leaned over and planted soft kisses on his chest, rubbing his abs in the process. I worked my way up and kissed his lips before softly nibbling on his lips. I felt him palm my ass and he opened his eyes.

In between kisses he managed to get out "Why... you... stealing... kisses?"

I didn't consider it stealing, those lips were already mine. Before I could respond, he turned over, putting me on my back. I loved the aggressiveness that came out of him when we had sex. Shit turned me all the way on. Cameron nibbled on my left nipple while he played with the other.

"Mmm, baby."

The throbbing I felt between my legs was becoming unbearable, and it was like my body was yearning for him. He knew that, but he wasn't about to give me what I wanted so easy; he rarely ever did. Cameron put one of my legs over his shoulder as his kissed down the center of my stomach, to my inner thigh. My body jerked when I felt him slip his tongue into my leaking opening. Shit felt too good. The way he worked his tongue felt like he was spelling his name on my shit; marking his territory I guess, but a chick wasn't complaining. He penetrated me with two fingers as he nibbled and sucked on my clit simultaneously. I couldn't take it. At that point I was trying to scoot away from his mouth, but he wasn't having it. Cameron pulled down on my thighs to hold me in place.

"Stop... trying... to... get... away." He said in between sucks.

I felt pressure start to build within me, and knew a climax was coming. I grabbed his head and held it as my legs began to shake.

"Fuckkkk, I'm cumin baby." I let out a long hard breath as I released all on his tongue.

Like the good nigga he was, Cameron cleaned up his mess; licked and slurped every drop of my juices. That nigga had a sexy as smirk on his face as he stood up and came out his briefs before lying back on the bed.

"Come ride daddy."

I didn't need to be told twice. I straddled him and slowly slid down on his piece. I had to give my pussy the chance to adjust to that nigga's size. It didn't take long though before I was slamming up and down against his thighs.

"Damn, baby!" Cameron called out.

I was on a cloud, and his words went in one ear and out the other. He grabbed my waist and bounced me faster. Before I knew it I was cumin again.

"Yesss, Cameron. Fuck this pussy baby."

Once Cameron let go of my waist, I turned around and rode him in reverse cowgirl. He slapped and grabbed my ass as I went to work. Before I knew it, he had pushed me onto my knees into a doggy style position, and was sliding in from the back. He pumped in and out, slowing down only to slap my ass. I threw my ass back to match each one of his thrusts.

"Who pussy is this?" He called out.

I gripped the sheets and moaned "Yours baby…this… pussy… belongs… to... you."

He grabbed my ponytail; not too rough, but rough enough to turn me on even more. I arched my back a little more, and he continued to hit my spot over and over. That nigga's pipe game took me to places I had never been before. He had me on clouds I didn't know I could reach. I felt another orgasm building up.

"Ohhhhh… Cum with me baby."

On cue, our bodies released at the same damn. That had to be the best feeling in the world. I fell face first onto the bed, and Cameron fell back. We laid in silence for a few minutes, waiting to catch our second wind.

"I'm going to shower baby. You coming?" I asked standing on the side of the bed.

"Yeah beautiful, give me a minute I'll be there."

I spun around on my heels and headed to the shower. By the time Cameron came in the bathroom, I was already getting out. I hoped he didn't think I was going to stay in there till I turned into a prune because he took forever. I kissed him as I walked passed him and headed into the bedroom.

After slipping into some comfortable clothes, I changed the sheets on the bed, then sat down and rolled him a blunt. He had taught me how to roll a few days ago. I wasn't a smoker, but I didn't mind having my man's blunts ready for him when he wanted one. I left the blunt on the night table next to his cell phone so he would be sure to see it, and headed to the kitchen to make breakfast. As I was standing over the stove making Cameron an omelet, I heard him scream out.

"When I catch you, I'mma fucking kill you, your mother, and your seed you bitch as nigga."

I turned off the stove and rushed to the bedroom where I found him cursing out loud to no one in particular, and getting dressed.

"Baby what happened?" I walked up to him and grabbed his arm.

Cameron said nothing, just continued to get dressed. He was in the process of slipping on his construction timberlands, when I stepped in front of him.

"Cameron, please don't start this. We been doing so well, and being open with each other. Let's keep that up."

He didn't seem fazed by my words as he grabbed his Moncler coat off the chaise that sat in front my window. He stormed out the bedroom and headed to the front door. I stayed on his heels. Before he walked out the door, I gave it one last try.

"Cameron, stop please!"

He turned around and I saw a look on his face that I have never seen before. I saw fear. He pulled me close and hugged me before passionately kissing me.

"I will call you and fill you in the first chance I get Skye. I just can't right now. I'm sorry. I love you."

And he was gone. My heart was racing. He had just told me he loved me for the first time, but the way things seemed in that moment, I worried it would be the last time. I became frantic and paced my living room back and forth until I decided to call the only person other than my parents and Cameron who could provide some comfort.

"ARIANA!" I screamed into the phone as soon as she answered.

Chapter Nine

Matt

When I got the call that this nigga was caught slipping, I almost hit some black flips on my Olympic shit. The day I'd been waiting for was had arrived. For the first time ever, I felt like things were going to work in my favor. I was on the first thing smoking back to the big apple. I wasn't missing that moment for nothing.

Man was busy at the spot, so he sent his uncle Max to pick me up from the airport. That was cool with me as long as I didn't have to catch a taxi. I know them shits were convenient, but trying to catch one as a black male was hard as shit.

****

When we pulled up to the location, I became anxious; that was my moment. I had always been the underdog, but not that day, though. Niggas was about to learn that you can't just shit on people and expect to have no repercussions. It was time for that nigga to pay up. I hopped out the whip and followed behind Max toward a house that looked to be abandoned. I felt a little uneasy because I didn't have a burner on me. I mean, I was cool with those niggas and all, but still. Shit, look at Max, that nigga was one of my father's top niggas, and he was partaking in taking his life. There was no loyalty in this business, and I was surprised my pops lasted as long as he did.

When we got inside the house I had to cover my nose, because the shit reeked of piss and all types of other shit. I was glad when Max opened a door which led to the basement. As we descended the stairs, the smell began to fade, and I moved my coat from covering my nose. The sight I laid eyes on was beautiful; shit made me feel like a little kid in the candy store. I mean, any other nigga probably would of shit on himself after seeing that shit. They had that nigga tied to a chair butt as naked. My pops' looked pretty bruised up, and blood was leaking from everywhere on the nigga's body.

"Ya'll went to work on this bitch." I said before hulk spitting on him.

"I was itching to kill the nigga, because they bodied my little brother! But I agreed to let you do the honors. My word is my bond. So I just whooped his ass every time I got the urge to kill him." Man said as he through water on him, helping to wake him up.

"Rise and shine, Pops." I said as I let out a demonic laugh.

All the niggas in the room was looking at me like I was crazy, but at that point, I didn't give a fuck. Those niggas didn't know my struggle, so I didn't expect them to understand.

"You not my son, you bitch ass nigga. Your mother was hoe! Maybe I would have claimed you if she got the DNA test like I asked. But her hoe ass knew you wasn't my kid. So fuck you. Fuck all y'all niggas. Cam gonna…"

Not only did this nigga disrespect my mom's but he had the nerve to mention his bitch ass son who wasn't around to save his poor daddy's life. I snatched the 9mm that was in Max's hands, and put a bullet right straight through his head, instantly ending his life. I watched his brain matter splatter, but that shit didn't faze me. In that moment I felt good, and I was ready to dead that nigga Cam too; not before I found out who his connect was though. I soon would be the nigga calling the shots.

"Damn son, why you had to kill him that fast." I heard Man say, snapping me out of the celebration I was having in my head.

"Fuck that nigga. He thought I was about to listen to him talk shit. I didn't come here for that."

As I was ranting, I looked over in the corner and saw duffel bags against the wall. I walked over and unzipped one of the bags to find neatly stacked bills.

"Where this come from?"

Max walked over to me and picked up one of the bags. "We were supposed to be heading to meet their connect to pay him some money, and get some more work."

"You know who their connect is?"

I watched Max shake his head no. "This would have been the first time he took me with him. Usually he took Rick."

Damn, I was a little disappointed but it was all good, I didn't mind putting in a little more work to get the results I wanted.

"This is $750,000, and $500,000 in each of those. Once we get to a safe spot we can split the shit evenly."

I never been around so much money in my life. I had the urge to kill all those niggas and keep the bread for myself.

I was smarter than that though, I needed these niggas; for now at least.

Man walked over to us with a lighter in his hand. "Let's burn this shit down."

I had a better idea. I walked over to his dead body and got his phone out his pocket. I scrolled through his phone book until I found the person I was looking for. I hit call and listened as it rung. When Cam answered I pointed to Man.

"Wassup pops?"

Man smirked and got closer to the phone. "Not your daddy, fuck boy." The line went quiet. "Cat got your tongue bitch?"

Cam finally spoke up. "When I catch you, Imma fucking kill you, your mother, and your seed you bitch as nigga."

He sounded tough but I knew he was shitting bricks.

"Oh yea? Meet me on the corner of Georgia and Linden; blue house."

Once he hung up, we bust out laughing. We was gonna let this nigga find his daddy with his brains blown out. He would be next that's for sure.

Cameron

When we pulled up to that house, I didn't know what to expect, but I was taking whatever risk; I didn't give a fuck. That was my pops life we were talking about. I would die in a heartbeat for that man. It was just me and Ty, because I didn't have time to reach out to anyone else. I could have made time, but that was the last thing I was worried about. We hopped out Ty's car and approached the run down blue house that that sat on the corner. We looked up and down the street before pulling out our guns and entering the house. The first level was quiet and empty. We trailed along the wall as we cautiously went up the stairs. We searched each room but there was nothing or no one.

"Fuck!" I yelled out in frustration.

"Calm down bro, we gotta be missing something."

He was right but what was it? Then it hit me. We headed down the stairs and opened every door until we found the door that led to stairs. I took a deep breath and looked over at Ty. He gave me a reassuring look that regardless of what was to come, he had my back. I knew that though. I hesitated, dreading finding out what might be down there waiting for us.

"I'm right here bro. I'm with you every step of the way. Go ahead."

I started down the steps with Ty behind me. When I reached bottom of the steps, I felt like my life had been sucked out of my body. I fell to my knees and looked on in disbelief. Ty was speaking, but I couldn't hear shit that was coming out of his mouth. I was trying to process the fact that my pops was gone. Brooklyn was about to feel like Iraq with the heat I was about to bring to the streets.

I felt like screaming. I was never one to cry, but in that moment, I could have cried a river. I had to hold it together though. I refused to look weak in front of anyone; even if it was just Ty. I saw Ty had knelt down beside me and I felt his arm go across my shoulder.

"Cam, I swear to you son we will get everyone responsible for this shit. I'mma go as far to include anyone who share the same last name as Man. You got my word, bro!"

I appreciated how genuine Ty sounded. I was very aware that niggas really couldn't be trusted in this game, but I trusted him whole heartedly. I didn't doubt that he would follow me to the end of the world to get these bitches back. I just hoped he was ready.

"I appreciate it bro."

What the fuck was I going to do about my father's body? I didn't want to leave him there like this, but I couldn't call the cleanup crew.

"Think Cameron, THINK!"

I had to yell at myself to remind myself I had to keep it together. I still had an organization to run. My time to grieve would come, it just wasn't right now. I stood up and paced back and forth as I gathered my thoughts.

"Aight, do me a favor, Ty. Go pick up Skye and take her to my mother's house. I promised her I wasn't going to keep her out the loop anymore, and I'm trying to stick with that. Don't tell my mother and Vic anything, except that I will be on my way."

Ty looked at me like he was confused. I wasn't in the mood for this nigga to get dumb founded.

"Bro, are you fucking crazy? These niggas just declared war. We don't know who we can trust anymore, and you think I'm about to leave you?"

He was right, fuck was I thinking?

"Cam lets go, from the car we can call the cops and say we heard shots, and let them find him. I know you don't want to leave him like this, believe me neither do I, but we don't have a choice. Unless you don't want a funeral and all that shit, we can bring in the clean-up crew. But we're not doing that to your moms. Let the boys get him to the morgue and shit, and we'll go from there."

Everything he was saying made sense, but I couldn't come to terms with leaving him like that; but I knew that I had to. I walked over to his body and kneeled down,

"I got you Pop, I promise man. I love you."

I felt a tear drip and I knew I had to get out of there before I had a complete breakdown. Before turning to go up the stairs, I grabbed my father's cell phone that was lying on the floor and left with Ty following behind me. Once we got in the car, I instructed him to pick up Skye and take me to my mother's house. Before he pulled off, I read the house number so that I could give it to the police. I was scrolling through my pop's phone book when I came across the person who could help me; Detective Harris. I didn't really fuck with cops, but my pops had a few of them on payroll. Harris reminded me of myself, which is why I didn't mind dealing with him. He was a street nigga who became a cop just to stay ahead of shit. Smart man, but at the same time dumbest nigga in the world. What street nigga was willing put himself around a bunch of pigs all day? It worked for him and our operation, so I couldn't complain about that. I hit call, and when he finally answered, I told him everything; starting with the phone call. Of course I left out the fact that I knew who it was. I mean, even though he was a dirty cop, he was still a cop and that shit would still be considered snitching. I just needed him to handle my father's body. He said that he would contact me when they need someone to come down and claim the body.

I really couldn't believe that shit happened. I must have been in denial all these years, thinking niggas on my team was loyal. Never would I expect niggas to cross my father like that. It's cool though, I had a surprise for those niggas. I was putting heat to every nigga who I thought could be a suspect. If they ever looked at my pops wrong, disagreed with him, or mumbled under their breath, that was their ass! I didn't give a fuck at this point. Niggas was going to pay.

Chapter Ten

Skye

When I got the phone call from Ty, telling me to come downstairs, I flew out the door. I was happy that I was already dressed; however, I wished I would have taken the time to mentally prepare myself for what was to come. As I approached the car, I noticed Cameron sitting in the passenger seat. He didn't even acknowledge me, but that's not what stood out to me though. As I looked into his eyes that were once full of life, I saw emptiness. What the hell happened? I climbed in the back seat of the truck and sat quiet. An eeriness flowed through the car, sending chills up my spine. Something was terribly wrong. There was no music playing, no conversation, no eye contact, nothing! I was left with no choice but to sit back quietly as he headed to where ever it was that we were going.

****

When we pulled up to the house, I remembered it from Thanksgiving. We were at Cameron's parents' house. I instantly got nervous; I hoped everything was okay with his parents and his sister. Those were the most important people in the world to him, and I didn't even want to imagine how he would handle anything happening to either of them. We were parked in the driveway for a good ten minutes before Cameron decided to climb out the car. He opened my door and reached for my hand. I slowly placed my hand in his as I got out the jeep. When our hands clasped together, I felt bound to him. It was a very satisfying feeling, but at the same time, extremely scary. I never felt connected to anyone outside of my parents and Ariana. This was on a different level though, he was hurting and I could feel his pain. He dragged his feet as he moved toward the front of the house, as if he carried the weight of the world on his shoulders. Something told me things were about to take a drastic turn. I didn't know if it was going to be for better or worse, but I knew that I was going to ride it out. Was I ready was the questioned I asked myself repeatedly.

When we finally walked into the home, we were greeted by his mother. Mariah was such a sweet lady. I only spent time with her on Thanksgiving, but we frequently texted and sometimes even talked on the phone. She had a heart of gold, and you could tell she went above and beyond for her family. She reminded me of my mother in that sense. I knew that if I could be at least half the mother they are to their children, to my own kids I would be alright.

Her warm, welcoming smile turned into a worrisome frown when she saw the look on Cameron's face.

Walking over to her only son, she hugged him while saying, "Hello Skye, and Tyquan. Baby boy, what's wrong with you?"

Cameron said nothing. Instead, he pulled out of her embrace and headed towards the steps. I needed to know what was going on, so I followed him. I followed him into a room which I figured was his old bedroom. It was extremely tidy to be the bedroom of a boy, but I guess that's because he didn't stay here anymore. I glanced around the room before closing the door, and sitting next to Cameron on the edge of the bed. There was so much I wanted to say, but I was afraid that saying the wrong thing would have sent him over the edge. Fuck it, though. I couldn't take sitting there in silence for another minute. I turned my body at an angle so I could attempt to look him in the eyes, but he wouldn't acknowledge me. I still needed to find out what happened.

"Cameron, baby what happened? You're scaring me." I prayed that he would answer me. It took him a minute but finally he slowly spoke. "They killed my pops baby."

Nothing could have prepared me for that moment. I literally felt my heart break into pieces. I hadn't known his dad for a long time, but time didn't matter. All that mattered to me was my man loss his father, an amazing woman loss her husband, and a young girl had to go the rest of her life without her father. What do I say? What do I do? No amount of words would be able to ease the pain he felt, so I didn't even try to talk to him. I knelt in front of him and pulled him close. The minute we embraced, Cameron broke down. I knew he was fighting back tears, and I felt good knowing that he trusted me enough to allow me to see him in such a vulnerable state. I rubbed his back as he sobbed. I knew Cameron was crying for not only his father, but for all the friends he loss and was unable to mourn.

When his cries stopped, I planted soft kisses on both of his cheeks then his lips. I knew he needed me; even if he didn't tell me.

"I love you Cameron."

Cameron looked at me and smiled. It wasn't the big smile that I was used to, but it was still sexy.

"I love you too, Skye. Look, I need you to understand that shit is going to be crazy from now on. My pops is gone, so not only do I have to handle the niggas responsible, I have to run this organization. Let's not forget it's a fucking snake running rampant that needs to be beheaded as well. I love you, and I want to be with you, but I'm not asking you to go through this with me."

Was he kidding? It's obvious that this is where I want to be. I could have walked away a long time ago. It's time for him to realize that I was there, and I didn't have plans on going anywhere.

"You don't have to ask me, Cameron. I'm where I want to be. What type of woman would I be if I left you when you needed me most?"

Before he had the chance to speak, his phone started ringing. Cameron looked at it and sadness fell over him once again, but that didn't stop him from answering.

Cameron

Although I was expecting Harris' phone call, it didn't make the shit any easier. Ty and I were gonna head down there and verify the identification of my pops body. But first, I had to tell my mom's and Vic. That was going to be the worse part of dealing with his death. I had to make sure my sister and mother were straight, and I knew they were gonna take it hard. I found a little comfort in knowing that I had a shorty who was going to stick with me through this shit. I just hoped that when shit really did go down, she would stand by her decision to ride.

"Go downstairs and take my mother in the living room. I'mma go get Vic from her room and I'll be down there." I said to Skye as I kissed her forehead, and headed out the room.

I dreaded every step I took toward my sister's room. Her and my pops were extremely close. She would definitely take losing him the hardest. When I got to Victoria's room, I tapped on her door.

She took a minute but finally said "It's open."

I opened the door and walked in. Vic was sitting in her window with her laptop on her lap, and phone in hand; probably on them social sites, because that's all she did.

"Wassup big bro. I didn't know you were coming over today." She squealed as she stood up to hug me.

My baby sister was my life. We were extremely close. We didn't have the normal brother and sister relationship, because we never argued, or disagreed. I could be dead ass wrong, but Vic was standing by me and vice versa.

"What's good mini me, come with me downstairs I gotta put you and mommy on to some shit."

I turned around and headed out the room, and she followed. When we got to the living room, we found my moms, Ty, and Skye chopping it up. I had the most important people in the world in that room, and I made a vow right there and right now that I wasn't losing none of them. Losing my pops was enough.

"You feeling better baby boy?" My mom's said, smiling up at me when she noticed me standing in the archway.

I took a deep breath and moved an inch closer. "Mom and Vic, I need to tell y'all something about Dad."

Her smile instantly turned into pain. It hurt my heart to see my mom's mood shift like that. Seeing her made me want to break down, but I couldn't. I had to be strong for my family. I was now the man of the house, and I had to maintain our life.

"This is all me! I can't be weak... I CAN'T BE WEAK."

Once I convinced myself that I could handle the responsibilities, I continued. "I just got a call..." I felt like shit that I had to leave out pieces of information, but I figured the less they knew the better. "Dad's was found, in an abandoned house..."

Victoria got up and stormed out the living room. Without me even having to ask her, Skye got up and followed her. I sat down next to my mother who was completely shaken up. She had been with my father since she was 15. He was her first, her only, and her everything. I knew she felt like her world just came crashing down around her. She had me though, and even though I couldn't bring my pops back, I had her. I was going to make sure she was good. I wrapped my arms around her and held her as she cried. Only god himself understood the physical pain I was placing on myself by trying to suppress cries, scream, and volatile behavior. As my mother calmed down, I explained that I had to go to the morgue. I hated that I had to leave my mother, but I had a load of shit to take care off. I texted Skye from the car, letting her know that I needed her to take care of my moms and sister until I got back. I felt a little better knowing that she would help console them anyway she could.

****

When Ty and I pulled up to the coroner's office, I had to reach deep within to drag myself out the car. Part of me didn't want to have to say bye to my father, but I knew I needed to get it done and over with so I could handle everything else. Once I stepped in the building, a chilling feeling flooded my body. Nah, it wasn't because the air was on; even thought that tripped me out because it was December. I guess the bodies needed to stay cool or some shit. Knowing that building was probably filled to capacity with dead bodies was creeping me the fuck out, but I was on a mission.

After signing in, I had to sit and wait to be called. Shit felt like I was there forever, but in actuality it was only fifteen minutes; fifteen minutes too long if you ask me. I was escorted to the room where my father's body was held, and they said I could go in or look through the glass. Since I knew it was him, and I was just doing this shit as a formality, I opted for the glass. I watched as the mortician pulled the sheet back. Seeing my father laying there with his eyes open with a tiny bullet hole in the center of his head enraged me. I had to get out of here. I nodded my head so he could cover him up, before returning to me with paperwork. I signed those shits with lightning speed and dipped.

Chapter Eleven

Ariana

When I got the text message from Skye about Cam's dad, a sense of guilt filled my veins. I felt like I should have spoken up when I realized what was up. How could I though? What would I say? And would Ty still have been involved with me? He was the first guy I'd been with in a while that really showed me that he cared, and just wasn't in it to hit and split. I didn't want to lose that. I know that if Ty and Cam found out that I knew something was going on and didn't share it, it would be not only the end of Ty and my relationship, but my life as well.

It's not like I had anything to do with it. Maybe they would understand the position I was in.

I cursed out loud. "SHIT!"

Why was I wasting time trying to convince myself that this wasn't going to end badly either way I put it. I fucked up and probably would suffer dire consequences because of that. I wished I could go back to that day. If only I could go back to that day...

****

I paced the floor as I thought about everything that took place that day. I was leaving the radio station after my shift. I host the late show, and usually didn't drive. It was a little after eleven, and I was standing outside my job, trying to flag down a cab. I was surprised to see my ex, Man hopping out his whip. He said he understood that I had a man and respected that he just wanted to see me and have dinner as friends. It was freezing outside and I didn't see a yellow taxi in sight so I took him up on his offer.

We ended up hitting this bar uptown for wings and drinks. It was cool, we kicked it about the brief relationship, and why it didn't work. I was never one to dwell on the past, but Man felt the need to tell me how he still felt like I was the one that got away. He could have told that story walking though. I don't digress, he had his chance and the shit passed. We were laughing, joking, and enjoying the music and shit when he got a phone call.

Man kept yelling "Unc chill. I got it covered."

I already knew the shit he was involved in, so that didn't faze me.

When he hung up he spoke to me. "My uncle Max be on some scary shit."

Of course at the time I didn't really put two and two together; not until Ty told me they were beefing with Man and his boys from Cypress. That's the same time I remembered that Cam's guard was Max.

"WHY THE FUCK DIDN'T I SAY SOMETHING!" I screamed as if someone was with me.

Chapter Twelve

Cameron

After the coroner's office, we headed to one of the warehouses we had in Brownsville. I needed to pick up the recording to the cameras, and something told me to scrutinize those shits because we were missing something. I learned a long time ago to go with my gut, and at that point, my gut was screaming at me; telling me to look at the recording.

When we got to the warehouse, everything seemed in place. Only people who knew about this spot was Ty, his pops, my pops, and me. If something was out of place, I would have definitely had to step to Ty, but it wasn't so I could relax; at least for now.

****

After we left the spot we headed to the city. I needed to hit up a few stores in SOHO to get Skye some clothes and shit. I wanted her to stay with my mother and Vic until I got to the bottom of this shit. I felt better knowing that they were safe and in the same spot. A select few people knew where the house was, so they should be good there.

As we headed back to Long Island, I thought about reaching out to some other niggas that worked for my pops. I felt like there were other niggas I could probably trust, but truth be told I wasn't trying to risk it. Ty and I would handle that shit on our own; at least until his pops, Jeff touched down. Jeff was out the country though, handling some shit in Panama, but he would definitely be ready to lay down a serious murder game when the news hit him about my pops. We decided to wait till he was back in the states to let him know, because he needed to be focused on the shit he was dealing with out there.

Skye

We were all laid out in Mariah's California King sized bed. I looked over at them sleeping. Instantly, a wave of sorrow went through me. I felt extremely bad that I couldn't do much to help ease the pain that Victoria and Mariah were going through. I did the best I could though. I made them some food, tea, and comforted them while they cried themselves to sleep. I really couldn't imagine dealing with the death of my father. The thought alone made me feel sick to my stomach. I needed something to take my mind off the madness that was going on. I picked up my phone and went to my kindle app. I remembered that I didn't finish *Love Lies and Obsession* by this new author, Demettrea. I thought about going downstairs, but decided against it. I wanted to be there if one of them woke up and needed me. After propping up a pillow, I got comfortable and dove into the book.

That lady was ill with the pen. I was so wrapped up in the story line that I forgot about what was going on around me; that's until Cameron came busting in the door. I raised my finger to my lip quickly, hushing him before he had a chance to wake them up. I was happy to see him. I had no clue what he went out to do, and at the moment it didn't matter. I was just glad he made it back safely. I slowly got out of the bed and walked out the room behind my man.

I pulled Cameron by the back of his shirt, stopping him in his tracks. When he turned to face me, I pulled him close and hugged him. Being in his arms felt so right. If I could have stayed in that moment forever, I would. He used his index finger to lift my chin, and kissed me.

"I love you, Skye."

I felt tears well up in my eyes, but as soon as they began to fall he wiped them away.

"Don't cry ma. I'm straight."

He was back to being Cameron with the tough ass exterior. I knew better though; he was far from straight. I followed him into his room where I saw a bunch of shopping bags on the floor. I was confused because he was supposed to be handling some business when he went out.

"Baby you went shopping?" I asked, walking over to his bed and sitting down.

"Nah, those are for you. I need you to stay here for now. Just until I ..."

I cut him off. He didn't really need to explain to me. I didn't want to be anywhere but near him in case he needed me. I also didn't mind being there for his mother and sister.

"No need to explain babe. I'll, stay and thanks for the stuff."

He stood in front of me, leaned over and kissed me. I wanted him; right then, in that moment.

"Baby, I gotta go downstairs and discuss some shit with Ty. Are you hungry or anything?"

Damn so much for the quickie I wanted to have. It was okay though because I understood he had a lot on his plate. It was my job to be understanding, so that's what I planned on doing.

"No, I made us something to eat, before they went to sleep. I'mma jump in the shower and just relax; probably finish reading. I'm here if you need me."

Cameron smiled at me, I was happy that through all of that, he could still manage to smile. I admired his strength.

"I love you beautiful."

I blew him a kiss, and watched him walk to the room door.

"I love you too."

Chapter Thirteen

Ty

While Cam was upstairs checking on his moms, sister, and Skye, I was able to have my moment. I knew not to cry or show how hurt I was in front of Cam. I had to be strong for my nigga, but truth be told I was hurting like shit. Hassan was like a second pops to me. He was the true definition of a real nigga, and a straight leader. He made sure everybody ate well, and didn't treat the cats who worked for him as peasants. Hassan was well respected, which is why that shit was so shocking. Who had big enough balls to cross him in that magnitude? Stealing from him was one thing, but killing him? There's no rock on Earth that the culprits could hide under. Cam and I were gonna hunt those niggas down and drop them one by one. Just thinking about that shit hurt my heart. I felt tears well up in my eyes and didn't even attempt to hide them. I let the tears fall.

When I heard footsteps approaching I wiped my eyes and sat up straight.

"Yo bro, come downstairs."

I looked up and saw Cam standing in the doorway. I really had to give it to that man. The way he was holding his shit together was shocking. I didn't know if I would have even been able to function if it was my pops.

"Aight." I got up off the couch and followed him down to the bunker.

"Son, we gotta watch this DVD, and I mean really watch it. These niggas are not that smart. They had to have slipped up. I just have a feeling the answers to everything are on the tape."

If my pops watched that shit and didn't see anything out of order other than the robbery itself, I doubted that we would. But I decided watch it to satisfy my brother's curiosity.

"Aight put it on."

There was a red leather sofa sitting across from the fifty-two inch TV that was holstered up on the wall. I walked over to the couch and sat down, propping my feet up on the table. After Cam put on the DVD, he took a seat on the other end of the couch. We were focused on the DVD that was playing. We watched as Max and Rick unloaded the money and the product from the car. Rick took everything inside to put away while Max stood guard outside. There was nothing out of ordinary except that somebody was always supposed to be on lookout while the other stashed the product and bread. Max made a phone call before joining Rick inside. Why didn't he stay outside? Cameron must have been thinking what I was thinking because he sat up and really focused on what was going on.

Minutes after Max went inside behind Rick, a black SUV pulled up; some old ass Durango. Four guys hopped out, and all of them were wearing masks except Man. Dumb niggas! After a few minutes of prepping their weapons, two of them headed inside, and that's when the shots started. We saw Rick run out of the warehouse, and was stopped dead in his tracks by the tip of Man's piece. We saw the gun flash and Rick dropped. As painful as that was to watch, we couldn't stop. My mouth nearly hit the floor as we watched Max walk out the warehouse with the other two dudes carrying the bags that were filled with the money and the product. I turned to Cam, only to find him pointing his nine at me with tears streaming down his face.

Cameron

"Son, what the fuck is your problem?" Ty asked.

Was that nigga about to sit there and try to play me for a dumb nigga?

"Fuck you mean what's my problem? Son your pops watched this video. He saw all this shit go down."

I watched as a shocked expression covered Ty's face as the truth behind my statement hit him like a ton of bricks. I wanted to believe that he had no idea the snake shit his father was on, but at that point, everybody was a suspect. Fuck that.

"Cam, you my nigga; my brother, son. I would never cross you or your pops."

A part of me wanted to lower my gun, because we was family. Why did it have to come to this? Why? I was battling with just letting him live until I got to the bottom of it, or just killing him off GP. He kept trying to plead his case.

"Cam, son why the fuck would I watch this with you if I knew the shit would implicate me? Think! I'm just as shocked as you bro."

Ty had a point, but I wasn't ready to put my gun down.

"Call your pops, and tell him I sent you to review the tapes from that night again. Ask why he lied."

I could see him contemplating on what I just asked him to do. He knew that if his father said the wrong thing, either both of them were dead, or I was gonna kill his pops. Either way, it was a lose-lose situation for Ty. But I hoped he would attempt to spare his own life.

"He still in Panama."

I looked at Ty sideways. "You trying to play me? This nigga getting money, thanks to my pops. I'm sure he can afford the fucking roaming charges. Call him!"

Good thing we were in the bunker, because the way I was screaming would have definitely woke up my moms and them. I watched as Ty pulled out his iPhone and called his pops. I prayed my boy didn't cross me. It rang four times before Jeff finally answered

"What up? You straight son? Why you calling me while I'm out of town?"

Ty hesitated, so I had to reposition my gun to remind him what was gonna happen if he didn't cooperate.

"Pops I gotta ask you something, and I need you to keep it 100 with me. Hassan was bodied today my man…"

Jeff cut him off. "I know you not calling to ask me if I had something to do with it when you know I'm in Panama."

There was all the proof I needed. That nigga didn't even seem fazed that his best friend was murdered.

"Nah, Cam sent me to the spot to check video from the night of the robbery. I watched the whole thing. Pops tell me you didn't have shit to do with this. Why you lie about what you saw on the tape?"

The line went silent for a minute. "Fuck them niggas, Ty. That nigga Hassan wasn't built to be no leader. He had us doing all the leg work while he reaped the benefits. Fuck that nigga and fuck Cam. You that nigga lap dog. He don't see you as his equal, but ya head too far up his ass to see that though."

I didn't want to hear anymore. I wanted to kill Ty because his father was scum, but he was my brother. I lowered the gun and sat back on the couch as he wrapped up the conversation with his pops.

"What now?" I heard Ty say as he ended the call with his father.

That's the same shit I was thinking. I mean, that was the ultimate test of our friendship. His father had to die.

"Ty, you already know. I'm going to kill Jeff. You either can live with that and just not deal with me, or kill me right now. Wait, nah that's not an option because your piece in your car. So you can live with the fact that your right hand man going to kill your father, or go to war with me at a later date. That's on you."

Ty

I couldn't believe it came to that. For anyone else, the choice would have been easy. Blood is thicker than water, right? It wasn't that simple though. My pops and Hassan grew up together, so how the fuck could he cross the man that always had his back? Then, he turned around preached that loyalty shit. I was disgusted and embarrassed that I had to call that nigga my father. I didn't share his same views about the situation. As far back as I could remember, Hassan was a team player. Yea, he may have had little niggas putting in work, but he was the boss. How did niggas expect that shit to go? It was too many chiefs, and not enough Indians. Everybody wanted to be the boss.

Cam on the other hand, was just like his pops. He looked out for everyone around him and kept his niggas straight. We never bumped heads, which you would expect since his pops was the boss man. You would think he would be on some *I'm above everyone else because my pops is that nigga* type shit, but he wasn't. He was in the streets with us, and he put in work with us. I couldn't even force myself to agree with what my pops said. One thing my pops told me, which was a statement that Hassan used to say all the time was that "Snakes needed to be beheaded." It's fucked up that the snake is my pops, but I knew what had to be done.

I looked over at Cam who looked as if he was in deep thought just as I was.

"Yo Cam."

I waited for him to look up at me. I'm glad it took him a minute because it gave me a chance to prepare my words in my head.

"I'm not trynna go to war with you bro. My pops went against the grain so he gotta pay the price."

Cam's eyes almost popped out his head. He didn't expect me to side with him. Shit, honestly I didn't think I would side with him either. That was my pops we talking about, but that didn't change the fact that he fucked up.

"Nah. Imma keep it trill with you Ty. I respect that you picked me over your pops. That's loyalty, and I wish all niggas had that shit flowing through them like you. But I'm not gonna let you agree to me killing your pops. I would never do to you, what your pops did to me. I tell you this though, he better stay where he's at. It's not enough space in the states for the both of us. If we cross paths, shots will be exchanged. He either gonna kill me, or I'mma kill him."

Chapter Fourteen

Cameron

I really did respect that Ty was willing to ride for me. He knew his pops had to get it because he did the unforgiveable, but I knew that Ty and I would never be able to overcome me killing his pops, even if we tried. I couldn't have that tension with him right now. Putting the bullshit aside with his pops, he was still the only nigga I could trust, and I still had problems that needed to be solved. Max was at the top of my list. When he started working for my father, that nigga was homeless. His baby moms put him out because he wasn't working, and she got tired of providing for the nigga. My pops cleaned him up and gave him a job. Never bite the hand that feeds you.

Man was next, his death was going to be slow and painful, but first I was going to kill everyone that he loved; his mother, his sister, and his daughter. He had to be last because he had to see how it felt to lose people that you love. I guess losing his brother wasn't enough. I wonder how he would feel knowing that Max was the one who pulled the trigger, sending his brother to an early grave. Niggas really didn't have an ounce of loyalty when money and power was involved. I knew that before but I was feeling it now in the worst way.

I looked over at Ty who was sitting in deep thought. He hadn't said anything since I told him that I was gonna let his pops live. I was fine with my decision because I knew that I would see him again, and when I did it was on sight. How did my pops do that shit on a daily basis? I was physically and mentally drained. I just wanted to lay up with my shorty and exhale.

"Yo, Ty, I'm ready to take it down for the night. On some real shit, I just want to relax get my mind right and shit. I'll get at you tomorrow to discuss our next move."

I didn't even wait for him to respond. I just got up and headed towards the elevator. He got the message and followed behind me. After letting him out, I headed upstairs to Skye. I had some frustrations that I needed to release, and I knew her pussy would be the best therapy. I walked in the room and found her passed out in the bed. I contemplated waking her up but decided against. I needed to figure out a way to show her how much I appreciated her. She lived a pretty normal life, and there I came, shaking up her world. But instead of dipping, she was still there. I walked over to the side of the bed and lightly kissed her cheek. I was about to walk away when I noticed a rolled blunt sitting on the nightstand.

I chuckled low, I loved shorty. She knew I was gonna need this shit after the day I had, and she had it ready for a nigga. I couldn't wait to blow that L, but I needed a quick shower first. After the shower I smoked my L, climbed in bed with my shorty, and got some much needed sleep.

****

Since the day of my pops death, I put everything on hold. All the niggas who worked for my pops reached out to me once they heard about his death, but I brushed them off. I didn't want sympathy, or help, or nothing! Even Max called me. That nigga had nerve, but I kept it together because before I dealt with him and everyone else, I needed to make sure home was together. Christmas was a week away, and the women in my life deserved to have a semi normal Christmas. It would never be normal again for my moms and sister because my pops' wasn't there, but I would do my best to make it comforting. Skye had been a big ass help around the house the past few days. She cooked, cleaned, and decorated the house in hopes of getting us all in the Christmas spirit. On top of that, she had two finals she had to take the other day that she didn't get a chance to study for.

I prayed she did well. Skye worked so hard that semester and managed to hold me down. I on the other hand, skipped finals. School was the last thing on my mind.

****

My alarm went off, shaking me out of my thoughts. I'd been up for a minute, but I just forgot to turn the alarm off. I grabbed my phone off the night stand, turned it off, and laid back down. It was the day of my pop's funeral. I wasn't ready and hadn't the slightest idea as to how I was going to get through it. I knew I had to hold it down for my moms and Vic, but telling myself I needed to do that and doing it, was two different things. I laid there in deep thought until Skye turned over and kissed me.

"I heard the alarm go off baby, get up."

Damn, I wasn't trying to wake her up because I really wanted her to sleep as much as she could. I low key had a feeling she was pregnant because every time we fucked recently, she couldn't take the whole thing, and she usually she handled the shit like a pro. Not to mention she hadn't needed those pad things for a minute. I didn't know though, maybe her cycle was fucked up or whatever other female issues chicks go through. I was sure she would tell me if she was pregnant, but just in case, I tried to keep her stress free.

"Aight beautiful I'm getting up," I said as I sat up in the bed.

"What time your parents going to be here?" I asked her while looking through the messages in my phone.

"They are going to meet us at the church because they are going to pick up Ariana. Speaking of Ariana, when I last spoke to her she was asking about Ty. She said he been calling her, but didn't want to see her and that wasn't normal. You know wassup with him babe? It is kind of weird that he hasn't even been over here in the past few days."

Shit, I didn't even tell Skye the shit that went down, and how I found out that Jeff knew that Max had set Rick up, and was working with the Cypress niggas. Why did she have to ask? I had been keeping my word about not keeping stuff from her when she asked, but I didn't want to indulge in that stuff at the moment. However, I decided to tell her anyway.

Chapter Fifteen

Skye

I couldn't believe the shit Cameron told me about Ty's father and Max. I had planned on taking a shower with him, but I couldn't get up. I had to lie there and really process it. That shit was real. When Cameron told me about his lifestyle, I didn't anticipate it would get that messy. Everybody wanted to in a position of power. I was really starting to question everything. Was it even worth it anymore? I had to shake that feeling. Regardless if it was worth it or not, I told Cameron I was going to stick with him and that's what I planned to do.

I climbed out of bed and headed in the bathroom to join my man in the shower. Seeing Cameron in there with the water falling off his body reminded me how much I loved him. When I stepped in the shower, he turned to face me and kissed me.

"I thought you wasn't going to come."

I didn't respond; no words were needed. I took the rag out his hand and washed him up. When I was done, he did the same for me. I lived for those moments, because they helped me answer the questions that I was asking myself earlier. It was definitely worth it.

After the shower we headed in the bedroom to get dressed. I was sitting on the bed applying lotion to my skin, as I watched Cameron put on his Tom Ford suit. My baby cleaned up nice. Once he was done getting dressed, he headed out the room. I assumed that he was going to check on his mother and sister. I was moving extremely slow because suddenly I felt sick. I figured it was because I knew I was headed to a funeral, so I brushed it off and continued to get ready. I slipped into the BCBGMAXAZRIA dress that Cameron picked out for me. I then, stepped into my black Christian Louboutin Daff pumps, and headed downstairs.

****

As our limo arrived at the church I kissed Cameron and whispered "I got you baby" in his ear.

It was important that he understood that I had his back and that he wasn't going through this alone. Yes, he had his mother and his sister, but they were in no position to comfort him. I was there for all for all of them. I watched as he stepped out of the limo first, and then took his mother by the hand. Victoria and I exited next, and followed Cameron and his mom into the church. I held Victoria's hand as we walked down the aisle to the front row which was reserved for family. Once they were seated, I kissed Cameron on the cheek and hugged the ladies. I didn't plan on sitting in the front with them. I was going to find my parents and Ariana, because that was something that they had to do together. When I went to walk away, Mariah stopped me.

"Where are you going? Please sit with us, Skye. You are family."

Mariah's words meant a lot to me. I didn't protest it, and took a seat next to Cameron.

****

The service was amazing, they sent Cameron's dad home in a very classy manner. Everything was breathtaking; from the flower arrangements, to the song choices performed by the choir, down to the speeches given by Cameron and his mother. During the service, I couldn't help but notice the amount of people that came out to say their final goodbyes to Hassan. You could tell that he was heavily respected.

When we got outside, something stuck out to me as odd just as Mariah and Victoria got into the limo. I noticed a group of about six or seven guys watching our every move.

"Baby," I said, tapping Cameron.

"Yea, what happened?"

I looked in the direction of the men and spoke. "Do you know them?"

When he saw who I was referring to, his face turned sour. He spun on his heels and headed in their direction. I contemplated getting in the limo, but decided that I was going to stand beside my man. I walked quickly so I could catch up with him. When I reached him, I took his hand in mine and squeezed it; had to remind him we were in it together.

"Young Cam," one of the guys spoke up.

He looked to be from some sort of Spanish descent; Mexican maybe.

"Miguel." Cameron said as he nodded his head at the guy.

The Spanish man looked at me and licked his crusty lips. That shit made my skin crawl.

"Who is this pretty lady?" His voice sent chills up my spine, but not the chills that meant I was turned on. They were the ones that made me want to run back to the limo to get away from his ass.

Cameron's nose flared up as he spoke. "My girl."

The Spanish guy who Cameron referred to as Miguel smiled. Ugh, who was that man? Before he could speak, Cameron spoke cutting him off.

"Thanks for coming to pay your respects. We gotta head out though and get to the cemetery."

We turned to head back to the limo when Miguel stopped us in our tracks.

"Cam, we didn't come for trouble. As you stated we wanted to pay our respects and to let you know we are now owed two million dollars."

Cameron turned red and started to speak.

"No need to object." Miguel said, stepping closer to him.

Cameron didn't back down either.

Miguel continued to speak. "You lost my money once, and I allowed you the opportunity to pay it back with your little interest. Now the money is late, and you didn't reach out to me. I see you have been dealing with a lot, but that doesn't have shit to do with my money. So as I stated, two million dollars, and you have two days. I would say tomorrow but I'mma give you a day to regroup after having to bury your father; but only because I like you. I must warn you that, if I have to take this trip again, it won't be this civil."

Miguel turned to walk away and the guys who were with him followed. Cameron said nothing, he just escorted me back to the limo and we headed to the burial site.

Chapter Sixteen

Cameron

When we got home from the burial site, we were joined by some of the guys who were really close to my pops, and even Max was amongst the men, but that was for my own reasons. Ty also joined us. Things had been awkward between us and I made a mental note to address that before the night was over. Even Skye's parents where there to show support, along with Ariana. I didn't want anything like that but my mom wanted to have them all over for dinner. After days of convincing me, I gave in. As her, my sister, Skye, and Ariana went to work in the kitchen, I gathered all my niggas and we headed to the bunker.

"I thank y'all for coming to pay respects to my pops. I appreciate it." I spoke as they all settled in.

Most of them were familiar with the bunker because like I said, they were the closest to my pops. As I walked over to the TV to start the recording, I heard some of them telling me that thank you wasn't necessary and shit. I nodded to the comments and pressed play.

I didn't need to watch it again; instead, I watched Max as he began to sweat bullets. Everyone except Ty, Max, and I were confused as to why I was playing the recording, but they would soon understand. As they watched Max walk out of the warehouse helping them Cypress niggas with the shit the stole, they all simultaneously drew they weapons and aimed it at their target.

"I can explain, Cam. It ain't even like that."

I walked over to him and punched him in his mouth. Max grabbed his jaw and winced in pain.

"Speak when I ask you a question." I barked.

I looked over and saw that J.R's piece had a silencer on it. I smiled at him. Knowing why I was smiling, he handed me the burner.

"So riddle me this. How you know Man? Why you set my pops up? AND who else is in on it? You got one chance and one chance only. Make it count."

I looked around at the other guys in the room and saw how they were looking around at each other. I silently hoped that Max didn't implicate anyone else in this room when he started name dropping.

"Answer me bitch!"

He gulped before opening his mouth to speak. "Man, is my nephew."

That nigga really was a snake. He killed Man's brother, his other nephew, and I didn't even ask him to.

"Nobody here knew what was up. Actually, no one else on the team knew. Rick started fishing and that's why he got killed. And as far as your pops goes, Man's plan was to take him out, take you out, and take over Brooklyn. I was going to be his underboss. Cam, nobody wants to be a driver or a security guard they whole life."

The fuck? Who would say some dumb shit like that when they about to see the light?

"Max, you a dumb nigga. You were muscle, and a driver, but you ate like a king and got greedy. Niggas like you don't deserve to run with real niggas son. What happened the day my pops got bodied?"

I don't know why I even asked that. The facts surrounding the murder didn't matter because it wasn't going to bring him back. I was curious to know though.

"I picked him up so that we could go pay the connect, but instead I took him to that spot to meet Man. Man sent me to the airport to pick up some other nigga, and I took him back to the spot. Your pops and the nigga said words, and he killed him. We took the money and dipped."

Other nigga? Who the fuck would kill my pops for Man? Shit was bigger than I fucking imagined.

"Who's the other nigga and what the fuck he had to do with it?"

Everything that took place proved exactly why Max was muscle and a fucking driver. Any real nigga would have taken his death like a real nigga. That bitch was in there singing like Beyoncé.

"He not from here his name is uh… Matt…Matthew, or some shit."

Ty and I looked at each other and our eyes said all the talking as Max went on.

"I don't know what he had to do with it or why he wanted your pops dead. All I know is that when he got there, he called your pops dad or some shit like that, and Hassan went off telling him how he wasn't his son and his moms was a hoe. That's when he shot him."

I heard everything I needed to hear. I raised gun and aimed directly between his eyes and got ready to end his life before Ty stopped me.

"Not like this Cam."

I looked at him strange. What the fuck did he mean not like this? "

"We about to go upstairs and have dinner with your moms, sis, your girl, and her parents. You want to do that with blood stains on our suits and gunshot residue on your hands? I know you ready to end his life; shit we all are, but not like this."

I hated that he was right. I was ready to off that nigga right there, and right then. That was one of the many times I was reminded why I was lucky to have Ty on my team.

"Aight, we'll go have dinner. Everyone keep your eye on this nigga, don't let him... As a matter of fact!" I reached in his pocket and snatched his cell phone. "Wouldn't want this bitch calling for back up. But yea if he moves, somebody better follow him. If he tries to leave, shoot him where he stands. I'll just have to deal with my moms and Skye's parents, but he's not living through this night."

I watched as everyone shook their heads in agreement and I dismissed them, keeping Ty behind.

"What happened? We good?"

Damn shit had gotten so sour between us that the nigga was acting all jumpy and shit.

"Calm down bro. I'm trying to find out if we're straight from you. Since that night, shit been different. You don't trust that I'mma leave your pops be unless we bump into each other, or you think I'm mad at you? Wassup?"

I needed to know where his head was at.

"Nah bro, it ain't even like that. I know your word is your bond. So when you said you gonna let my pops rock, I didn't second guess that. It's just different. I mean now we know my pops didn't have anything to do with the murder but he still was disloyal, and that shit doesn't sit well with me. And I do feel like you may feel some resentment toward me because of him."

Did I feel resentment toward him? Nah, for what? His pops made his decisions, and Ty was his own man. I couldn't hold him responsible for another man.

"It's different because we making it different. You my nigga, Ty. I don't feel no way towards you over that shit. If we going to get those niggas, we gotta put that shit behind us bro for real. We even got heat coming down on us from Miguel and them niggas, and I need you bro."

Ty's face scrunched up when I mentioned Miguel. He knew going to war with them Mexicans was a recipe for disaster; hopefully for them.

Ty stuck his hand out and we gave each other dap as he said "I got you bro."

We headed upstairs, while I told him what went down at the church with Miguel.

****

Dinner went well; even Max pretended to be enjoying himself. I guess he wanted his last few hours on Earth to be peaceful. I was glad Skye's parents were over. I know she missed them, and I felt bad that I had been taking up so much of her time that she didn't get to see them. Skye's parents were understanding and felt that she was just trying to be supportive while we dealt with the loss of my dad. I mean that wasn't a lie, but it wasn't the entire story. After dinner, when Skye's parents left, my niggas and I headed to the spot in Brownsville. I wasn't trying to be out there all night. I wanted to get this shit done with and go home to my favorite girls, which is why as soon as we got there I ended that nigga life. Why waste more time? I watched the cleanup crew do their thing and Ty took me home.

Chapter Seventeen

Matt

After the nigga Hassan's funeral, I spotted Cam talking to some Mexican niggas. I knew they had to be his connect. Those niggas looked like big money, and moved like bosses. Not the type of bosses that was running around the hood; more like the niggas you see on TV. I knew approaching them would be a huge risk, but fuck it I had to take my chances.

Once I seen Cam's limo dip, I caught up with the Mexicans. Of course, they didn't want to hear shit I had to say, but I had some information that would make them listen. I told them about the money we took when I killed Hassan. Of course I told my version of how shit went down; leaving out the fact that I killed Hassan. Actually, I left the incident out altogether.

The bullshit ass story I made up must have sounded believable because they told me to take a ride with them. Of course, I was hesitant at first. Mexican niggas ain't shit to fuck with. They are the definition of seven thirty, which meant they were absolutely crazy. During the ride they told me how they were going to handle the Cam situation, and offered me his position once he was out the picture. Shit was sweet. Not only were they doing the dirty work, I was still getting everything I wanted when I set out on this mission. Shit was coming together nicely. I was feeling like Lil Wayne *"I ain't got no worries."*

Chapter Eighteen

Skye

I jolted out of my sleep when my alarm started blaring in my ear. I stopped it quickly before it woke up Cameron as well. He got in late last night, so I knew he wanted to get some rest. I rolled over, frustrated that I had been woken up out of such a good sleep. I contemplated going back to bed, but I know I needed to keep the appointment with my doctor. The last week or so I'd been feeling extremely crappy. I hadn't had energy for anything, nor did I have an appetite, and my boobs were sore as fuck. Not to mention the last time we tried to have sex, it hurt like hell.

All those were pregnancy signs, I know, but I'd been in denial about it since I missed my period twice! Don't get me wrong, I was happy as hell about becoming a mother, but I just wished the timing was better. With all that had been going on; the beef with the Mexicans, and not being able to catch Man, I already had to worry about my safety when I was in the street, but now I had to worry about my child.

I glanced at the time, and decided that I needed to get up and get ready because Ariana would be picking me up soon. We hadn't had any time together since before

Cameron's dad's death, so I reached out to her to accompany me to the appointment. She was excited as hell. I couldn't front, so was I. The entire time I was in the shower, I thought about my baby. How was he or she gonna look? What were we going to name him or her? How was I going to be as a mom, and Cameron as a dad? As I was getting dressed, my phone vibrated and I saw that it was a text message from Ariana.

I'm outside bestie, hurry up. I hope your ass is ready and not have me sitting outside forever.

I had to laugh at her because she knew me too well. I was indeed still getting dressed, but after getting her text I moved faster. Once I slipped on my Uggs, I wrote Cameron a note telling him I was running out with Ariana, and I left. When I got outside, I hopped in Ariana's car and I instantly hugged her. Even though we spoke every day, it wasn't the same as seeing her in person. I truly missed my best friend.

"Hey Bestieeeee!" I said, stretching the word bestie to add dramatics.

She laughed. "Hey chica."

I frowned, realizing what was playing through her car speakers as she pulled off. I hadn't ridden in her car in so long, I had forgotten that Ari listened to classical music in the morning. Don't get me wrong, I did love to relax to Bach, but in the morning I needed some hype music to help me start my day right.

"You know this not gonna work girl," I said as I pressed the radio feature, switching to Power 105. Monica's "Love All Over Me" was playing. I sang along, thinking about Cameron.

****

When we arrived at my doctor's office, I felt butterflies. I don't know why I was nervous; I already knew what it was. I just wanted my doctor's confirmation, as well as a checkup to make sure everything was going as it should have been. After signing in, Ariana and I sat down and waited. I picked up one of the brochures on pregnancy and started to read through it, when I felt my phone vibrate. I took it out my pocket and saw that it was a text from Cameron. I smiled, knowing that he was checking on me.

Wassup baby. Why you didn't wake me up before you left. Are you okay? Did you eat?

Seeing that I was right about him checking on me, I laughed as I texted him back.

You came in late and I wanted you go get some rest babe. And yes I'm okay. I will grab food before I head back home. I love you Cameron.

When I was finally called to see the doctor, my nerves started to get the best of me. Maybe I should have brought Cameron along with me after all. Nah, it was okay. He would be able to come to every appointment after this one, so I wasn't worried. My OBGYN was a sweet lady. My Doctor was so personal with her patients; she didn't treat us all the same, and tended to our individual needs. That's what I loved about her. When I entered her office, she decided to talk about life, school, and everything else before jumping into the reason I was there.

As I already knew, the pregnancy test she performed confirmed that I was pregnant. I was going to be a mommy. No words could express how I was feeling. I was on a cloud, and out of all the shit that was going wrong lately, I now had something to smile about every day, regardless of what was going on, and Cameron did too.

In addition to having lab work done, I got a pap smear. I had already mentally prepared myself for that stuff. I just hated needles. After the exams were done and blood was drawn, the doctor and I had a discussion about my medical history, and she gave me a bunch of information about what I could expect. The best part of this visit was finding out my due date, which was August 13th. I would look forward to the day I get to see my precious baby's face. It was such an amazing feeling.

****

After the doctor's appointment, Ariana and I headed over to Beauty and Essex for some food. It was a new spot that my mother told me about, so we decided to check it out. It was a nice place, and we loved the atmosphere. It was a nice mix between a bar and a restaurant. The food was good, and we would have loved to try their drinks, but I was pregnant and she was driving. I definitely would be trying them in six months.

I had to admit that it was a much needed day out with Ariana. I had a chance to take my mind off the madness, even if it was only for a few hours. I just needed a minute without having to think about pissed off connects, ungrateful ass snakes, revenge, and all the other shit that was going on. I'm not saying I had a problem being there for my man, because I didn't. I just missed normalcy. I missed my damn condo for sure. I loved being at Cameron's mom's house with them, but I missed my space. I couldn't express these concerns with Cameron though because he already had a lot going on. It felt damn good to express them to Ariana. As always, she was a shoulder and a listening ear.

Cameron

While Skye was out, I had a chance to make some phone calls. I had a fucking man hunt going on. I put two hundred and fifty thousand racks on each of them niggas heads, yet no one had any new information on Man and Matt. If those niggas was after my spot, I knew they didn't disappear. They wouldn't, not until they got what they wanted or until I killed them. Killing those niggas was definitely my intent.

"Where the fuck are these niggas?" I asked out loud to no one.

The shit was aggravating me. My organization needed to move forward. Niggas were hitting my phone, complaining about how they getting low on product left and right. To top it off, I was out of a connect. Could shit get any worse at that point? I had Sky there like a fucking hostage. I didn't let her go back to her crib, and she rarely saw her parents or went out. I knew that shit was eating away at her, but she was trying so hard to show me that she was a rider that she didn't say anything. I sensed it though.

****

I was in the middle of smoking a blunt when Skye walked in the room. She didn't even come all the way in, she just waved and turned around. I figured she was going to chill with Vic. They had become extremely close since Skye had been staying there, which was good. Who wouldn't want the most important women in their life to get along?

When I was finished smoking my blunt, I left out the room and went downstairs into the living room where I found all my ladies on the couch watching a movie. I sat next to Skye and pulled her close to me. I loved the shit out that girl. It had only been five months and she was riding with a nigga like we was married and shit. A basic bitch would have been left. I knew it was something about that girl when we first met.

Chapter Nineteen

Skye

The past few days had been good, with the exception of morning sickness kicking my ass, and me trying to hide it from Cameron. I wasn't trying to hide it because I was afraid of his reaction. I just wanted to surprise everyone when they came over for Christmas, which was only a few days away. I think he knew something was up because before I found out I was pregnant, I would roll his blunts and chill with him when he was smoking, but now I would exit the room fast, coming up with some lame excuse.

****

Christmas Eve rolled around and Victoria and I had to head out to shop for last minute gifts while Cameron and Mariah went food shopping. We went in four stores trying to find something for Cameron. He had everything, so it was tough trying to find things that I knew he would love.

"Skye, this is the last store we looking in for that fool. It's a shame we couldn't find something faster." Vic said as we walked into the Hermes store.

I laughed and nodded my head. "Okay Vic this is the last stop for Cameron, but girl honestly I was pressed to come here so I could get me a bag."

Victoria looked at me and bust out laughing. "Me too."

I joined her in laughter as we slapped fives. We had so much in common. We liked the same music, and had the same fashion sense. It made shopping with her much easier since we agreed on everything.

We browsed through the men's section, and I ended up getting him a bunch of things that I knew he would look good in. When I noticed Victoria lingering in the women's department, I went and purchased the bag she was looking at minutes before, along with the matching belt. She was going to be surprised and I wanted to make her smile. After leaving the Hermes store, we had to quickly decide on things for my parents, Vic and Cameron's mom, Ty, and Ariana because we had to beat Mariah and Cameron home. They didn't know we went out to get more gifts.

****

When we got home, we didn't see Mariah's car so we knew they weren't back yet. We were in the clear. We didn't have any wrapping to do because the store we went to did gift wrapping as they packed the stuff. All that was left for us to do was put everything under the tree, and we did that in no time.

Victoria wanted to bake cookies when we were done, but I really felt a little drained. I promised to keep her company while she made them. She moved around the kitchen getting the ingredients together, then sat across from me at the table. As soon as she opened the cookie dough, I got sick to my stomach and my food was threatening to come up… Nope it *was* coming, so I got up and ran to the bathroom.

I was standing over the toilet, holding my hair up as the food I consumed earlier came out. I felt like shit. I didn't think I could get with seven more months of that sickness shit. When I was done, I turned around to go to the sink and Victoria was standing there staring at me.

"Please don't ask me. Please don't ask me." I thought to myself.

"You pregnant, Skye?"

Of course she would ask me. Why couldn't a person have a stomach bug without it being a pregnancy? Vic was smart though, so I couldn't even try to fool her.

I smiled "Yes you're going to be an auntie!" I said stepping, over to the sink to rinse my mouth out.

She hugged me so tight that I thought she was going to squeeze the life out of me.

"Oh my gosh! Congrats, Skye. Does Cam know? How far you? When did you find out? Like, tell me everything."

I had to laugh at her, her intentions were good and I know she was excited, but she had to slow down.

"Slow down Vic. Cameron doesn't know. I planned on telling everyone tomorrow. I just found out a few days ago, and I'm almost three months."

Vic was smiling from ear to ear. I was happy she was excited, and I knew that she would be a great auntie.

"Vic is it okay if you make the cookies alone? I want to lay down for a bit until my parents get here."

She nodded her head up and down. "Of course girl, and I won't tell anyone. I think the Christmas announcement is a good idea."

I hugged her "Thank you."

****

My intentions were to lie down for a little while until I got my second wind, but I ended up falling asleep.

"Wake up baby." I heard Cameron say as I was opening my eyes.

"What time is it?"

He looked at his watch and said "9:30."

Damn I slept the whole day away.

"I would have left you sleeping, but I wanted you to get some food in your system."

Him mentioning food make my stomach turn. "I'm not really hungry baby. I'm going to get in the shower. Are you coming?"

Cameron leaned over and kissed my forehead. "Nah, I'm going to finish helping my mom's but when you done showering, come eat."

I brushed him off, climbed out the bed, and went to shower. I didn't know if it was the shower head, the water pressure, or a combination of both but that shit felt like sex every time I got in. After I was finished washing up, I wanted to stay there and enjoy the water massage, but I knew Cameron would come get me out the shower so I could stuff my face. It made me smile though, because he really cared about my well-being. I imagined how he was gonna act when I told him about the baby.

I stepped out of the shower and after drying off, I stepped my feet into my fuzzy slippers and put my robe on. As soon as I walked in the room, I saw a salad and a bottle of water on the nightstand. Cameron must have known that I was getting right back on the bed. I guess since he went out his way to bring it up I would try to eat the salad. I prayed that it sat right with me because that throwing up shit is for the birds.

Surprisingly, that salad hit the spot, and it stayed down so that was a plus. I took the garbage downstairs and climbed right back in the bed. Cameron, Mariah, and Victoria were in the kitchen slaving and I was in the bed watching Lifetime movies. I felt myself getting sleepy so I texted Cameron.

I'm getting sleepy and I want to lie in your arms. Can you come to bed?

He didn't text me back, but was upstairs in a minute flat. I waited up while he took a shower and as soon as he joined me in bed and cuddled me, I was out.

****

"Merry Christmas Chica!"

I knew that was Ariana's voice but why was I dreaming about her. I felt someone shake me softly and I slowly opened my eyes, and laughed.

"Merry Christmas, Ari. I thought I was dreaming girl. Y'all here early."

She sat on the edge of the bed, "I know, your mother and my mother wanted to be here early to help Mariah cook and stuff."

I loved that our mothers got along so well. We had really become one big family; which would be really official once the baby was born. I smiled and rubbed my tiny belly.

"Ty here already too?"

She nodded up and down. "Yup. Him, your dad, and Cameron outside playing basketball."

Now when my father came in complaining about knee pain and shit, he was on his own.

"Oh and Mariah said we doing gifts after breakfast, so get up and get your life chica."

When Ariana left the room, I got up out the bed feeling refreshed, and got myself together before heading downstairs and having breakfast with the family. When I walked into the dining room, everyone was there except me. Even the guys had wrapped up their basketball game. I spoke to everyone before sitting in the empty seat next to Cameron. There was so much breakfast foods on the table, I was silently praying that the smells didn't make me sick. So far I was good.

Everyone made their plates, then Mariah said grace and we dug in. After breakfast, we all gathered in the family room and exchanged the gifts. Victoria got all teary eyed when she opened the Hermes bag and belt I got her. I was happy to see her smile, because she deserved it. Everyone else received extremely nice gifts as well, and was happy. Once everyone opened all of their gifts, I was ready to make my announcement. I stood up and placed my things on the floor and on the couch next to me.

"I have a gift for the entire family; one that we can all share for years to come."

I started laughing because they were all confused; except Ariana and Victoria of course.

"I'm pregnant."

Whoa... everyone was more excited than I was, and it was my baby. The amount of support and encouraging words I received from everyone was overwhelming. I even started tearing up, but I blamed that on hormones.

"Mariah, we're going to be grandmas!" I heard my mom saying she hugged Mariah.

Cameron hugged me and didn't want to let me go. The rest of the day was so awesome. It was good for everyone as we played family feud, Pictionary, ate some more and just enjoyed each other's company. It was truly what we all needed.

Chapter Twenty

Ty

Wow, Skye really pregnant. I was happy for my niggas Cam and Skye. Becoming parents has to be about the best thing that could happen to you in your lifetime. I was not a father yet, but when I became one I knew it was going to be the best shit I ever experienced. Their baby was coming at a good time because they needed the joy in their life right now; well, Cam definitely did.

Sin City was having a Christmas bash and it took a lot, but I convinced Cam to go with me and Ari that night since we spent the whole day with the family. He needed to get out the house because you could see stress and worry all over his face, and that wasn't like my nigga at all. A nice not outing around bad bitches and fat asses should do the trick. Of course we couldn't touch the hoes, but we could watch and spend a little money.

****

When we pulled up to Sin City, the lines were long as fuck. Good thing we knew the niggas throwing the shit because we didn't do lines. We walked into the spot like we owned the shit. It felt good to be out on the scene with my right hand and my girl. It was a much deserving night out. Even though Cam wasn't trying to leave Skye home, I was glad he decided to come out. He going to be a father, which definitely called for celebration. What was a better way to celebrate than to ball the fuck out at the strip club?

The spot was packed with wall to wall people. We were barely able to get through to get to our table in V.I.P. In addition to it being crowded, people were stopping Cam left and right, giving him condolences for his pops, or praising his pops. It was appreciated but it wasn't the time or the place. My nigga just wanted to chill and celebrate the journey he was about to embark on. As his right hand man I was gonna make sure he had a good time.

"Son, what bottles you want?" I yelled in his ear as we settled in our section.

"Get whatever."

I could tell in his voice he wasn't really feeling being out. He was on edge since we now had beef with the Mexicans. I understood that and shit, but you can't stop living. I tried to tell him we were gonna see them Mexicans. We were going to see Man and Matthew too. Them niggas were gonna get theirs, but in the meantime we were celebrating the creation of life. Fuck it. YOLO!

"Baby I'll be right back." Ariana yelled as she walked down to the other section of the club.

I watched her every move until she caught up when some chick. I assumed she knew her by the way they hugged and were laughing. I tapped my pockets and remembered that I had a pound of Kush and was ready to roll up. Time to get high this nigga needed to cheer up.

"Yo, Cam roll up. I'mma go to the bar." I said as I handed him the fronto leaf and the bud so he could roll up while I went to order bottles.

I intended on going straight to the bar, but French Montana's "Freaks" came on and made me wanna rub up on some ass, so I set out in search of Ari. When I found her, she already knew what I was coming for. She walked over to me, turned around and started grinding her ass on me. My dick got hard.

"Damn Ari."

She was lucky we was in the club because I feel like fucking her pussy up. When the song ended, I gave my shorty a kiss and left her chilling with her friend. As I got closer to the bar I noticed six niggas who stood out like sore thumbs.

"Mexicans?" I said out loud to myself in disbelief.

Suddenly, a burst of gunfire erupted and the club went bananas. I pulled out my piece, ready to bust back when suddenly it felt like the time had stopped, and everything was moving slowly. I looked toward the V.I.P section where I left Cam, then to the dance floor where I left Ariana. I had a choice to make; go have my brothers back and make sure he was straight, or get Ariana to safety.

I said a short prayer for Ariana as I maneuvered through the frantic crowd trying to get to Cam. It was a hell of a task dodging bullets and pushing through the crowd, but I had to make sure my brother was good. I ran backwards, letting off shots in the direction of the Mexican niggas.

"The fuck man?" I yelled as if someone could hear me over the screams and cries.

These niggas weren't letting up. I had to take cover for a second behind one of the booths to switch the clip for a fresh one. Once I was good, I was up and on the move again.

"Cam where are you?" I kept saying to myself.

Suddenly, the gun fire ceased, and the Mexicans ran out of the club as quickly as they came in. I had finally made it to the V.I.P section.

"Nooooo!" I yelled out as I watched Cam choke on his own blood.

I fell to my knees next to him trying to see where he was hit. I tried to stop the bleeding, but it was too much; he was hit at least six times.

"Stay with me fam. We going to get you out of here."

Fuck the not crying thing, that be strong shit went out the window. I rocked my nigga back and forth and cried.

"You gonna be good, Cam."

It was not supposed to happen like that. I rarely called on God because I felt I wasn't deserving after the shit I'd done, but I had to.

"God, not him. He got a family he has to be here for and a baby on the way. Not Cam! Please."

I hoped God would help me out. Do me this one solid! I couldn't sit there waiting and hoping any longer. I got up and held Cam up by putting one of his arms around my shoulder.

"I got you bro. Just stay with me."

I didn't know if he was conscious, but I wasn't giving up hope. By then, the club had cleared out drastically so I was able to get around. Cam wasn't light, so I wasn't able to move as fast as I hoped, but I was moving. I spotted Ariana sitting on the floor covered in blood and crying.

"Ariana!" I called out to her.

I watched as she tried to stand, but something wasn't right. Ari was holding her stomach and blood was just leaking. Fuck she was hit too. I couldn't just leave her. I made my way over to her, still holding Cam up and held her the same way on the other side of me.

"Y'all stay with me. I'm going to get y'all to the hospital, just stay with me."

I heard Ariana's breaths. They were short and faint, but I heard them, and that's what mattered. Cam…not so much. I didn't care though; I was getting them to the hospital. We finally made it to where I parked my truck and I put them in the backseat the best way I could without causing more injuries. Ariana was alert she was crying out in pain.

"Relax baby you going to be okay. Do me a favor, talk to Cam. It doesn't matter what you say, just talk to him and keep yourself alert for me ma."

Ari did as I told her. I jumped in the front seat and sped off. I didn't give a fuck about getting pulled over; this was life or death.

****

I swerved into a parking spot in front the emergency room entrance of Bronx Lebanon hospital. My car was crooked, but that shit didn't matter. I jumped out the car and rushed inside, returning with doctors, and got Ariana and Cam on gurneys and rushed them inside. I tapped my pockets looking for my phone, but the shit wasn't there. I walked over to my whip and looked for it, but it wasn't there either. Fuck man I needed to call Skye.

I walked into the emergency room hoping that the nurse at the nurse stations would let me use the phone. After explaining to her that I needed to contact their family, she let me. I called Ariana's parents' house; luckily the number was easy as fuck, and I was able to remember it. After speaking to them, I had to call Skye.

Matt

Niggas got lucky tonight. My little homie Chris hit my jack when he spotted Cam and Ty pulling up to Sin City. I was happy as fuck. I'd been keeping it low ever since I found out Cam put a price tag on my head. I didn't even know how those niggas found out about me. Miguel had me staying at one of his spots in the city until the Cam situation was handled. But after those niggas rushed out there with all that heat, I was sure the situation would be handled. It was my time, and I was ready to claim what was rightfully mine from the beginning. Only thing is that now I planned taking everything; even his bitch.

Chapter Twenty-One

Skye

I was on my way back to bed after waking up to use the bathroom for the fourth time, when my phone started ringing. I knew it had to be Cameron or my parents, because no one else would be brave enough to call me at that hour. I sat on the edge of the bed and answered the phone.

"He-llo" I answered, clearing my voice a little.

I removed the phone from my ear and looked at it strange. First of all it came from a number not associated with anyone in my phonebook, and the background was loud as fuck. I was pregnant, aggravated, and tired! I was in no mood for the bullshit.

"Hello!" This time I shouted.

"Sis…"

It sounded like Ty but I couldn't really hear through the noise.

"Ty?" I questioned.

I listened as the guy breathed heavy in the phone sounding, as if he was jogging. The noise seemed to decrease as well. I figured the caller was going to a place where we could hear each other.

"Sis!"

It was clear that it was Ty.

Why the hell was he calling me? Probably from the club that's why it was so damn noisy.

"Yes, Ty. What happened?"

The line went quiet. It seemed as if the longer we sat on the phone in silence, the more I began to panic.

"Tyquan!" I barked at him.

"They shot them sis. They fucking shot them. This is bad. Ariana will be okay, but I don't think he's going to make it. They shot my brother, sis. They fucking shot him!"

I knew that Ty was speaking because I heard him, but as far as knowing what he was saying, I didn't have a clue. The moment he said they shot them, everything went numb and my senses went blank.

Why was this happening? As if enough bad shit hadn't happened recently. I had to get to the hospital. I needed to see him. This had to be a dream.

"Skye are you there?"

Physically I was, but emotionally I was somewhere else. I'd say in limbo because if I lost Cameron...

"What hospital?" I tried to keep it together. For the sake of my child, I had to.

"Bronx Lebanon."

I hung up the phone. My brain was saying get up and put on clothes, but my body wouldn't listen. I could no longer suppress the urge to cry and I exploded. I let out a piercing scream.

"Why is this happening?" What am I being punished for?" I yelled out loud, not taking into account that Victoria and Mariah were sleeping.

I cried, and I cried hard. In between sobs I prayed, he had to make it. The thought of bringing our baby in the world without Cameron made me breakdown. Mariah and Victoria walked through the door and rushed to my side. At that point I was crying and repeating "Why Cameron?" Mariah began to panic as she tried to calm me down so that I could tell her what was going on. The thing was that I didn't know what had happened. All I knew was that, we had to get to Bronx Lebanon!

Victoria walked into Cameron's closet and came out with a pair of his sweats for me. I was still unable to move but she did the best she could at helping me put them on.

Everything was moving fast, I was dizzy and couldn't really focus. I fought with myself to get it together, and told myself that I could do this. If I learned anything from Cameron, I learned how to be strong. In that moment something hit me, whether Cameron made it through this or not, I would never be the same. In addition to that, whoever was responsible for causing all the havoc in our lives lately now had to deal with me. I stopped crying and got strength in knowing that I had to protect my baby, this family, and my man's organization by any means necessary.

****

After I got myself together, Mariah and Victoria threw on clothes and we headed to the hospital. When we walked into the emergency room, a feeling came over me. I felt it right there; Cameron was gone. Although I had that feeling, I still found myself walking over to the nurse's station demanding to see him.

"I need to see Cameron Carter!" I yelled at the nurse.

I felt a little bad for being nasty with her because this wasn't her fault but I was in no mood to be apologizing, fuck that.

"Ma'am, are you family?"

Was that bitch serious? Would I be in the emergency room at three in the morning trynna see a nigga who didn't mean shit to me?

"What room?" I asked, completely ignoring her question.

The Nurse sighed. I'm sure she dealt with shit like that on a daily basis, and you would think she would be a bit more compassionate.

"I'll get his doctor."

I watched as the ugly ass nurse went to get the doctor. I looked around for Mariah and Victoria, and saw them sitting with Ty who was covered in blood.

I began to move my feet and head in their direction until I heard someone call my name.

"Skye!"

I turned in the direction of the voice and saw Ariana's parents. I felt like shit. There I was, so worried about

Cameron that I didn't even ask about my best friend; not even once. I justified it by telling myself I didn't ask because Ty said she was going to be alright. Deep down, I knew it was still fucked up. I walked over to them and hugged her mom. She looked as if she'd been crying for days. Ari's mom's eyes were so puffy, they looked to be swollen shut. Her father looked as if he was hurting, but he was barely keeping it together for his wife's sake.

"How is she?" I manage to get out.

Her mother was still shaken up and couldn't answer me. I completely understood that. Her father, on the other hand, was able to explain to me her condition. I was relieved to know that she was expected to make a full recovery. Although I was extremely happy that she was going to be okay, I couldn't really show that because I was still one hundred percent worried about the fate of Cameron.

"Family of Cameron Carter?" I heard someone say.

I turned around as I felt my heart sink to the bottom of my stomach. Mariah was approaching the doctor. I jogged over to where she was standing with him. She was fighting tears, and seemed as if she was unable to get out her words, so I spoke up.

"We are Cameron's family."

The doctor's demeanor instantly changed, as sorrow fell over his expression. I said a silent prayer, for my baby, and for the families of the people who I was going to personally put under the ground.

As the doctor began move his lips, I heard… "We did all that we could, I'm sorry…"

CPSIA information can be obtained
at www.ICGtesting.com
Printed in the USA
LVHW011955021219
639196LV00003B/429